His Second Chance

Montgomery Ink Legacy

Carrie Ann Ryan

His Second Chance
A Montgomery Ink Legacy Romance
By: Carrie Ann Ryan
© 2024 Carrie Ann Ryan

Cover Art by Sweet N Spicy Designs

All content warnings are listed on the book page for this book on my website.

Praise for CARRIE ANN Ryan

"Count on Carrie Ann Ryan for emotional, sexy, character driven stories that capture your heart!" – Carly Phillips, NY Times bestselling author

"Carrie Ann Ryan's romances are my newest addiction! The emotion in her books captures me from the very beginning. The hope and healing hold me close until the end. These love stories will simply sweep you away." ~ NYT Bestselling Author Deveny Perry

"Carrie Ann Ryan writes the perfect balance of sweet and heat ensuring every story feeds the soul." - Audrey Carlan, #1 New York Times Bestselling Author

"Carrie Ann Ryan never fails to draw readers in with passion, raw sensuality, and characters that pop off the page. Any book by Carrie Ann is an absolute treat." – New York Times Bestselling Author J. Kenner

"Carrie Ann Ryan knows how to pull your heart-strings and make your pulse pound! Her wonderful Redwood Pack series will draw you in and keep you reading long into the night. I can't wait to see what comes next with the new generation, the Talons. Keep them coming, Carrie Ann!" –Lara Adrian, New York Times bestselling author of CRAVE THE NIGHT

"With snarky humor, sizzling love scenes, and brilliant, imaginative worldbuilding, The Dante's Circle series reads as if Carrie Ann Ryan peeked at my personal wish list!" – NYT Bestselling Author, Larissa Ione

"Carrie Ann Ryan writes sexy shifters in a world full of passionate happily-ever-afters." – *New York Times* Bestselling Author Vivian Arend

"Carrie Ann's books are sexy with characters you can't help but love from page one. They are heat and heart blended to perfection." *New York Times* Bestselling Author Jayne Rylon

Carrie Ann Ryan's books are wickedly funny and deliciously hot, with plenty of twists to keep you guessing. They'll keep you up all night!" USA Today Bestselling Author Cari Quinn

"Once again, Carrie Ann Ryan knocks the Dante's Circle series out of the park. The queen of hot, sexy, enthralling paranormal romance, Carrie Ann is an author not to miss!" *New York Times* bestselling Author Marie Harte

HIS SECOND CHANCE

The rules were simple. Protect the woman I love. And try to stop loving her along the way.

Kane Montgomery Carr and Phoebe Dixon's romance went from a fiery temptation to a fizzled out heartbreak.

Only Kane has no idea why.

All he knows is that he has to keep her safe when a stalker sets Phoebe in their sights.

Yet as the two of them are forced once again into each other's lives, the truth behind their breakup surfaces and they are forced to face the facts: the feelings and heat they buried aren't quite as gone as they'd like.

If they give in, they'll have to face the demons that broke them up in the first place—including a startling secret that shocks them both.

Yet if they don't, they might lose the chance of a life time.

That is, of course, if they can survive what lurks in the shadows for them both.

Chapter One

Phoebe

Then

I knew one day I would die. That the monsters of my nightmares would creep into my days and suddenly I would be taken from this earth. Perhaps the monster would be time itself and I would be old and happy. My family would surround me and I would not be alone.

Or it could be the other nightmare where I was eaten by a bear because my friend wanted to go hiking, and here I was, waiting for a bear to eat me.

"Tell me again why I'm out here in the middle of the forest waiting for a bear to rip my face off. Or perhaps a mountain lion. Or a snake. Or an armadillo." My voice went a little high-pitched, and my roommate and best friend Claire just looked at me, raising a brow.

"We're in Colorado, not Texas. You're not going to be bitten to death by an armadillo. Not that armadillos eat people." She frowned as she said it, as if not sure she was telling the truth. For all she knew, there *were* man-eating armadillos that only lived in the mountains of Colorado.

I narrowed my gaze at her, my lips twitching as I held back a laugh. "You don't know that. Perhaps at night when you think they're just rummaging around for bugs or whatever in people's yards, they're actually looking for ways to infiltrate your house so they can eat your eyes right out of your sockets as you're sleeping."

Claire tripped over her own feet and nearly landed face-first on the rocks. She caught herself, hands out, as she looked over her shoulder and glared at me.

"You're having a waking nightmare about bears, and suddenly you want me to have a weird eye-eating armadillo phobia? Are you serious right now?"

I shuddered even as I thought back to my words and held out my hands to keep Claire steady. "Okay, perhaps that was a little ridiculous, but it's really not my fault."

"Just because you say that in a high-pitched voice doesn't actually absolve you of any responsibility."

Claire grabbed onto my hand and squeezed and I just

laughed, shaking my head.

An older couple walked by, walking sticks in hands, and they glared at the two of us.

I didn't know if it was because we were holding hands, or that I had just yelled about armadillos trying to eat us.

"There are children here," the older woman said, and Claire tangled her fingers with mine.

No, Claire and I were not a couple—we had never wanted to be a couple. In fact, neither one of us was attracted to the other. However, if this woman had a problem with us holding hands, we weren't going to stop.

"Really, speaking of gouging out eyeballs? What would your children think?" The woman clucked her tongue at us and continued to walk, her husband rolling his eyes behind her.

Claire dropped my hand, her shoulders shaking as she held back a laugh.

"Well, at least that disdain was because I'm a monster rather than anything else," I muttered under my breath.

"Oh, I would fight to the end of the world for you for your rights, but not for your fetish about giving me nightmares." Claire wiped her hand on her jeans again since she had fallen back on a rock behind about a mile back. Of course, I had fallen right before her, so it wasn't that she was klutzy, we both were. So going on a hike in the mountains on a public trail where there were countless others watching us be idiots? A totally correct move.

"Okay, let's continue this monster of a hike," Claire grumbled and I laughed, releasing her arm as we made our way down the path.

I loved living in Colorado. I loved the sun on my face, the cool breeze from the mountains, and that I always knew where west was. It was a little hard to get lost when the mountains were always to the west. Unless you were *in* the mountains, and then you never actually knew where you were. Thankfully this was a state park that was embedded next to a national park, so there were plenty of signs. This wasn't one of those hikes where we needed a full backpack of supplies and tents.

In fact, this "circle" of a trail was only supposed to be three miles, except I hadn't actually read the intermediate-to-expert level badge on the map until we were already at the second mile marker.

"Three miles one way, but then the circle doesn't actually end where you began. How is that a circle?" Claire asked, her breath coming in pants just like mine. We were in shape, well at least as in shape as you could be without being an actual athlete. But the high altitude and rocky hills we were climbing weren't exactly easy. Then again, the older couple hadn't seemed out of breath. Maybe we *weren't* in as good shape as I thought.

"Seriously though, it's beautiful outside, and I'm really glad we did this."

I grinned over at my best friend. "It is. I'm happy that we're out here. Even though I know sitting at our favorite café eating cake would probably be a lot more fun."

We had two favorite cafés, one in downtown Denver called Taboo, and the other called Latte on the Rocks. Latte on the Rocks was a newer place and was apparently connected to our favorite place in downtown Denver. We hadn't even realized that until we had been there a few times and then connected the dots. It seemed that we had a favorite for a reason, and now I was craving an oat milk latte with butter pecan flavoring and a cupcake. Any cupcake would do at this point.

"You're thinking about more cupcakes, aren't you?" Claire asked, as I put my hand over my stomach.

"You want to take a break over in that seating area with the picnic tables? Eat the lovely trail mix we brought, that is not cupcakes, before we make our way back down the hill for this so-called circle."

"Technically it is a circle. It just takes the same number of miles to get here as it does to get back. Which is not what the trailhead said."

I shook my head, annoyed with myself for misreading the map, as we hiked our way the few hundred feet to the seating area. There were a couple of families there, though no young children since this hike was a little harder for them. And for us apparently.

I sat down at one of the tables that looked as if it blended directly into the environment and rested my feet against a rock. "This is going to suck going back to the car."

"Tell me about it," Claire said as she heaved her small pack onto the table between us.

We each had a small day pack just with snacks and water, but no other provisions. Not the smartest thing in the world, since maybe a first aid kit or a walking stick would've been helpful, but it was fine. It was still early in the day, and really, it wasn't that far of a hike.

We just hadn't been expecting it to be this challenging.

I pulled out our waters while Claire pulled out the trail mix, and we sat with our backs to the trail, watching the hawks fly overhead and the sun shine over the glistening mountaintops.

"I'm glad we're not hiking too high."

I turned to Claire. "I think this is high enough. But you're right. I'm glad there's no snow."

She shuddered. "Once with my roommate from college," she began, and I cut her off.

"Let's not discuss Tina, shall we?" I asked, holding back a shudder at the thought of Claire's former roommate. The woman had been intolerable: never did the dishes, always snuck her laundry into Claire's, and would have such loud sex at all times during the day and night, that Claire couldn't focus on anything in her own home. I mean, it was nice for Tina because the woman sounded like she was having fun, but she also had sex all over the house, whether Claire was home or not.

"Anyway, I went on a hike with Tina and her boyfriend at the time, and I brought a guy I was seeing."

I put my hand to my chest. "Gasp. A guy! Who was he?"

Claire flipped me off and I smiled. I was a little more sarcastic than Claire was, but of all of our friends, we were the two most soft-spoken and shy unless we were together. It was just how we were with each other.

We had been friends for ages, though we hadn't roomed together in college. We had gone to the downtown university, and while there were some dorms, I had lived with my family to save money, and Claire had a roommate. Now that we were adults though, with adult money and adult problems, we lived together to save some of that adult money.

"Are you going to let me finish this story?" she asked.

"Maybe. Maybe not."

"Anyway, this guy was like, oh let's go for a walk, and

my guy, though he was only my guy for that afternoon because hello, I have the worst taste in men."

"I feel like I am worse, but continue," I said with a laugh.

Claire shook her honey-brown hair before pulling it back into a tight ponytail. As the wind picked up, I pulled my long dirty-blond hair into a tight braid, annoyed with myself for not doing it earlier. Now it was going to be a tangled mess that I would have to deal with at some point.

"Thank you very much, but now I've forgotten where I am in the story."

I winced. "Let me see, the short walk wasn't too short, and you were with Tina and a couple of guys."

"Right, and no, the short 'walk' ended up with us having to trudge through a freaking tributary where there was snow."

My eyes widened. "Are you serious? How have you never told me this story?"

Claire blushed. "Because it was so stupid. The guy, well Tina's guy, gave us trash bags for our feet and we were supposed to just trudge away without getting frostbite."

"And you did it?" I asked, incredulous. We were *not* the hardcore hiking type of people—contrary to this morning.

"Yes, and my socks got wet, and everything was gross,

and I thought I was going to die, and then we were walking up this mountain in the cold and everything sucked. And it wasn't even actually winter. It was spring when the snow was melting, but we were so high up it didn't matter."

I shuddered. "We really aren't hiking friends, are we?"

"No. And we should be because we are in Colorado. But we don't ski or snowboard or do anything of the like."

"There are things to do in Colorado other than those."

"Maybe, but I feel like an idiot."

"Well, I promise not to force you through snow this time."

"At least this trail has public bathrooms at the end."

"And we're here eating decently yummy trail mix sitting on picnic tables on a trail that is well maintained. And we've already seen two park rangers walking around. No walking in icy tributaries or lakes."

"We were wearing tennis shoes."

I grimaced. "So, you really thought it was a *walk*."

"He didn't say hike, he didn't say mountains. He said a *walk*. And it was a nice day so I thought it would be fun. I was an idiot."

"Did Tina stay with him?"

"They're married and have two kids. They're happy, and I bet you they go on hikes where they're all prepared for whatever comes next."

"Well, at least we're wearing the right shoes this time," I said as I gestured towards our hiking boots.

"I learned my lesson. A little."

I grinned and popped another cashew into my mouth before rolling up the bag and stuffing it inside Claire's small backpack.

"I'm ready to head back, are you?"

"As ready as I could possibly be," she said with a shrug.

"Don't worry, we can do this."

She raised a brow.

"If I sound optimistic it's because I know we're close to being done."

"We're halfway done. Hence the edge of this circle."

"We both know that this geometry doesn't make any sense," I grumbled, before we stretched a bit and made our way down the path.

We walked past couple after couple, watching as they leaned on each other, laughing and stopping to take photos. When one couple asked me to take a photo of them, I did, with the perfect backdrop, and I couldn't help but feel a twinge of envy at the love in their eyes. Oh, it might not be the big L for them, or maybe it was. I couldn't tell.

I was the absolute worst with men, perhaps only second to Claire.

I knew there were plenty of men out there, I saw them all the time. And they were always married, douchebags, or only wanted sex. While I liked sex, sex was fun. But I would like some dinner and conversation along with the sex. Or maybe someone to just hang out with. Maybe someone to go on a hike with. No, scratch that, no more hiking for a long time.

I just wanted to be with someone.

"You're thinking hard," Claire said as we hiked our way down the path.

"I'm just a little in my feels."

"There are so many couples on this path."

I loved when our minds were on the same page without discussing it. "Right? I hate it. I mean, I shouldn't hate it, because it's just jealousy asking to be slapped in the face. But it'd be nice to actually have a long-term relationship."

"We are both catches, how come we can't make it work?"

"Because everything sucks, and we suck?" I asked, and Claire rolled her eyes.

"Really?"

"Okay, we don't suck. Well, I could make a dirty joke there but I won't."

Claire snickered.

"I just want to be happy. And to find a nice, rugged

man who can hold me against the wall as he pounds into me."

Claire burst out laughing as another couple walked by. Thankfully they hadn't seemed to hear what I said, and I counted that as a win. "Well, maybe we can get back on the dating apps, and we can add that into your bio. Looking for a man to rail me into a wall."

An elderly couple walked by and glared at Claire. I held my laughter in until they walked away, laughing so loudly that Claire just flipped me off again.

"How come you get people overhearing you talking about eye-eating armadillos, and I get *that*?"

"Because life is funny that way. And I don't know if I want to do a dating app again. I just want to find someone organically."

"And how are you going to do that when your job is literally helping couples design their dream homes?"

I winced, but she wasn't far off. I was an interior designer, and tended to help couples who had the means to hire an interior designer. Or I helped bachelors with too much money that didn't want anything to do with someone working for them. Which I totally understood, but still, it would be nice to meet a man who didn't treat me like a servant or some plaything.

"My job isn't much better," Claire continued. "I'm a party planner who usually deals with parties for couples or for work events where I'm so busy I don't get to breathe. And don't even get me started on the *weddings* I help with. No single men for me."

"And we're not the bar hopping crowd."

"When did we get old?" Claire asked, and I held back a snort.

"We're still in our early twenties, dear. Don't call me old. You know my siblings will kick us in the teeth for that."

I had four older siblings—three older sisters and an older brother, and I was the baby. Always the baby. It wasn't usually a big deal, and I was used to the way they treated me, always caring, always making sure I was okay.

"Maybe we should go bar hopping," I said, slightly determined.

Claire nearly tripped over another rock. "Are you serious?"

"We should get out there. The perfect man isn't going to just show up at our doorsteps or on this trail. We should go meet people. Not at work, and not at a coffee shop."

"Maybe at a coffee shop; there are some really hot tattooed guys that come in and out of that place."

I blushed at that, thinking of a few I had seen. "Most of them are married and work either at the security company or the tattoo shop next door." Our favorite new local establishment, Latte on the Rocks, was in the same strip mall with a few other businesses all in one building. There was even an art exhibit and studio in the end unit. Of course, I hadn't ventured into anything except for the coffee shop. I was nervous about getting a tattoo, and I didn't really have time to look at art, nor the money to pay for it. While my family was well off *enough*, I was trying to get out of student loan debt and trying not to rely on my family money to make life work.

And, thankfully, we hadn't had to use the security company at the other end of the building. Though I wasn't quite sure what kind of security they did. For all I knew they were bodyguards for celebrities, and that I was not.

"Are you saying you want to get out and go meet a man at a bar so we can actually be happy and find someone, or just to annoy your older sister?" Claire asked, and I narrowed my gaze at her.

"How do you know things before I even think them?" I asked.

"Because I love Isabella, but she is always on your case. More than your mom."

"Isabella likes to control everyone, because that's what big sisters do." I loved my older sister. She was fierce, amazing, and always fought for us when sometimes my mom couldn't. Oh, I loved my mother, her free spirit and how she made the world a better place, but she also never stood up for herself, only for her kids. Isabella tended to do all of that and more.

And that meant that whoever I wanted to go on a date with in high school, Isabella rather than my mom had been giving him the stink eye. Kyler, of course, my brother, also tried to step in as the big brother who took over the world and everything else. But Isabella was the one in charge.

"Okay, I'll go bar hopping with you if you actually do it. But we both know that we're both very much chickenshit."

I laughed at Claire's words, because they were absolutely true.

By the time we finished the walk, plans for our crawl were made, though I knew it wouldn't amount to anything but a long night, and perhaps some fun.

My legs hurt, I was thirsty even though we had a little bit of water left in our bottles, and I was ready to go home.

"What do you say to cupcakes and coffee at Latte on the Rocks?" Claire asked as we made our way to the final part of the trail, the parking lot in sight.

"That sounds perfect."

Claire pointed towards the bathroom to the side. "I'm going to head in there, do you want to join?"

I raised a brow, and Claire blushed.

"I meant do you want to go stand in line with me."

"No, I'm okay. You're the one with a bladder the size of a pea."

She rolled her eyes and went inside. I stayed on the side of the trail, the trees at my back, enjoying the view of the mountains to the west.

We were still around five hundred feet from the parking lot, and I was in the forest, and everything felt exhausting and thrilling at the same time. The hike hadn't been planned, but I was glad we had done it. I felt good.

And then I heard the crunch of twigs behind me.

I froze, nervous, and I tried to turn without looking like I was turning. I thought maybe it was just a man, some guy walking through the forest, or perhaps it was a serial killer, but not the very large black ball that I saw out of the corner of my eye.

My eyes widening, I turned and, off in the distance but far closer than it should have been, one of the nightmares from my dreams filled my vision, and it wasn't an armadillo.

"Bear," I whispered, barely a sound coming out as my mouth moved.

"Bear!" I said a bit more loudly.

The bear didn't look toward me, it just scratched its black body against a tree.

All thoughts of what I was supposed to do if I saw a bear fled my mind. Was I supposed to act big, was I supposed to stand still like a Tyrannosaurus rex? No, this wasn't a T-Rex, they could see movement, or they could see you even if you were standing still. This wasn't a brown bear, so they weren't as dangerous. Black bears were cuddly. But as I watched that claw dig into the side of the tree, I swallowed hard and took a tentative step back, and then another.

I was a few hundred feet from the parking lot, and the bathroom, but as somebody screamed behind me and slammed the bathroom door shut, I realized I hadn't been the only one to see the bear, and there was no way they were going to let me in.

So, I did the only thing that I thought I could do, because I was not a fight person, I was apparently a flight person.

This was probably the wrong thing to do in this situation, but I hadn't paid attention when they told you what to do if you saw a bear.

I ran.

I ran towards the parking lot, but our car was on the other end, and I could hear crunching and scuffling behind me. I had no idea if the bear was following me or if it even saw me. But it could probably outrun me. And it could kill me with a single bite.

Why couldn't it have been an armadillo that happened to migrate to Colorado?

Without thinking, I ran to the nearest car, even though it wasn't my own, and prayed it was unlocked. And when the handle moved I let out a relieved breath, nearly crying as I jumped into the passenger-side seat and slammed the door behind me.

The bear moved through the trees, then over the picnic area, as people scrambled away, some using their phones to take video, others being smart and getting away. The bear didn't seem to mind, and it calmly walked through the trees again, going unseen.

I didn't realize my breaths were coming in pants, and my hands were shaking, until someone cleared their throat beside me.

That's when I remembered that this wasn't my car.

I turned to see a large man in a beat-up bomber jacket and bushy beard looking at me as if I'd lost my mind by getting in his car without asking. I was a stranger after all, and had probably set myself up for not only humiliation, but being tied up and thrown in the back of his SUV.

The bearded man with blue eyes smiled at me and raised a brow.

Well, either I had jumped into a stranger's car and he was now laughing at me after I had run from a bear, or this was the second part of my nightmare.

I had just gotten into a car with a serial killer.

And yet, the serial killer felt like better odds than the bear.

"Well, that's one way to meet someone. You doing okay? The bear is gone. I'm Kane."

Would serial killers introduce themselves like that?

I cleared my throat. "Phoebe. Phoebe."

"Hello, Phoebe Phoebe."

I shook my head, then ran my hands over my face. "I'm just Phoebe. And thank you for saving me from the bear."

He shook his head, still smiling. "I didn't do a damn thing. But I'm glad I kept the door unlocked. You okay though? I didn't realize that the bears came so close up here."

"Neither did I." I ran my hand over my chest. "My friend is trapped in a bathroom. I should probably go check on her."

Kane looked at me and smiled. I swallowed hard, wondering why that smile did things to me.

He *had* to be a serial killer.

"Let's go check on your friend. And mine, since he's trapped in the other bathroom. Come on, Phoebe Phoebe. I'm glad you're okay."

I hoped he wasn't a serial killer—though it was still better odds than the bear.

Right?

Chapter Two

Kane

Well, this day had just gotten a bit more interesting. I looked over at the woman with the gorgeous blue eyes and long strawberry-blond or maybe dirty-blond hair pulled back into a messy braid. Those eyes had a bit of fear and mortification set deep, and I leaned back in my seat, grateful to have taken my seatbelt off earlier.

My cousin Kingston and I had come out for a hike, and then I'd gotten a phone call from one of my clients at Montgomery Security, and he needed to call family as well. Then everybody had started screaming, running away like there was an actual bear running after them, and while the bear had rambled around, it hadn't seemed interested in people. After all, we were on his land, invading his property, so he would've had the right to swat those giant paws at us. Thankfully it had been a black bear not a brown bear. I hadn't gotten out of the car, though I had been on alert at the first sound of trouble, had my hand on the door, ready to jump out of the car if needed. I wasn't armed, since we were on state park property next to a national park, and my concealed and carry permit didn't allow me to carry in parks.

I was in security, and was one of the top bodyguards we had. And that wasn't just me bragging on myself. I was the one they called when they needed to keep another person safe one-on-one. Kingston was too. Some of my cousins were better at electronics or setting up perimeters. Some could organize a group of eighteen and keep everyone exactly where they needed to be, when they needed to be there. I was better at one-on-one work. Mostly because I could smile and make the person I was keeping safe feel like they were actually safe.

None of that mattered right in that moment though, because there was a stranger in my car, a car I hadn't locked because I had still been in it, and Kingston had just gotten out.

"So, Phoebe Phoebe," I started, and she narrowed her gaze at me. That was good. The anger or frustration and irritation was better than the outright fear from before.

"Just Phoebe. You don't need to tease me."

I shook my head. "Didn't mean to tease you." That was an outright lie.

"Anyway, now that I am sitting here in a stranger's car, and you could possibly be a serial killer, I'm just going to go now. Please let me go."

Well, the reality of the situation sank in. And while I knew I wasn't a serial killer or anything of the like, getting into a stranger's car like that probably wasn't the smartest thing for her to do. I nodded and gestured towards the door. "The door is unlocked. The rangers and everyone are going into the forest to go look for the bear, so we should be safe. Where are you parked?"

"I don't think I should tell you that. In case, you know..." her voice trailed off.

I grinned. "In case I'm a serial killer, got it. Come on, how about we both walk to the area where your friend and my cousin are, and we figure out what's going on. I promise I don't bite." I hadn't meant for the words to sound so sultry, but she raised a brow.

"I'm pretty sure that's a lie too. But still, your bite would probably be better than a bear's." She blushed so prettily, I just smiled.

Today had gotten interesting. I really hadn't wanted to go on this hike. If anything, I had wanted to sit on my couch with a beer and watch sports and just do nothing. I wanted to be lazy and sit in my underwear and pretend that nothing mattered. We'd had a long case, one that had nearly killed Kingston, and the ramifications of everything that occurred weren't over yet. Daisy was still healing from the explosion, and I was tired. So damn tired.

Kingston was healed enough to go on this small hike and had dragged me along with him. And whatever he needed, he got. He had almost died, and I hadn't been there...I pushed those thoughts from my mind and opened my door.

"Come on. I'm not going to hurt you. I'm just glad that my door was unlocked for you to escape."

She sighed and opened her door, getting out when I did. "I can't believe it was unlocked. I would have kept trying until eventually I found my car. Of course, Claire has the keys in her bag, so that really wouldn't have helped anything. I guess I could have broken into it, but that would have taken time since I have no idea how to do that, and the bear would have gotten me by then."

Pink darkened her cheeks and she looked damn adorable. *And lickable. Time to think of something else.* "Claire's your friend?"

"Yes. And her name isn't Claire Claire," she said dryly, and I threw my head back and laughed.

"Look at you, you've got this down. Everything's going to be fine."

"I don't know if I actually believe that, but thank you.

It's just been a very weird day. Our tiny little hike turned into a strenuous one, because I didn't realize the circle wasn't a true circle."

I winced. "A lot of people make that mistake on this one. We did the first time we were up here," I said. She narrowed her gaze at me, probably because she thought I was making fun of her.

"Well, now I have to go make sure that Claire still isn't trapped in a public bathroom, which I don't even want to think about, and then get home and pretend this never happened."

"It'll be a story to tell though. How you wrestled a bear and risked it all to save a stranger."

She gave me a dry look. "Is that the story you're going with?"

"Hey, it could have happened. You never know."

"There was no wrestling. There was just pure panic. I wasn't even sure if I was supposed to get big and scare the bear away or run and save myself. Apparently I am a flight and not a fight."

I shrugged. "What they told us in movies as kids probably wasn't the right thing. None of us know what we're supposed to do with bears, because bears don't even know what they're going to do with us. Though that black bear was probably more scared of you than you were of him."

She blinked slowly. "I highly doubt that."

The doors to the bathroom opened then, the rangers telling everyone that everything was safe. I saw Kingston scowl at me, and then look between Phoebe and me, curiosity in his gaze. A woman with shoulder-length hair and a bright smile came forward; she had the same look on her face.

"Phoebe? Are you okay. The ranger said that nobody got hurt and that the bear is off doing its own thing, but oh my God. We were trapped inside the bathroom, and the Amazon holding the door wouldn't open it so I could let you in." Claire scowled at the woman who had to be over six feet tall as she confidently strode to her car on the other side of the parking lot, oblivious to the fact that she had probably scared Phoebe's friend half to death.

"I'm really okay. I'm just glad you were safe in there."

"And where were you? I had the keys. I felt terrible."

Kingston lifted his chin at me, and I did the same. There, we both knew we were safe, there was no need to go into it. But now I really wanted to know what was about to happen in front of us. I was bored. So help me.

"Oh," Phoebe finally answered, that pretty blush staining her cheeks again. I'd like to see exactly where she blushed all over.

"Well, I sort of got into Kane's car because he had the door unlocked, and he didn't murder me, so I count that as a win."

Claire blinked at Phoebe, and then looked at me. "You're Kane."

I grinned, absolutely entranced at this whole situation. If the bear had been anywhere close to Phoebe, it would have been different, but now I felt like we could sit back and laugh about it. "Yes, it's nice to meet you. Don't worry, your friend was safe. The bear wasn't even looking at her."

"That's not what it felt like when I was trying to run for my life," Phoebe snapped, and I lifted up the side of my mouth in a smile.

"Okay. If you like."

Kingston snorted beside me but kept quiet.

"Seriously though, he was kind not to kick me out of his car and call me a lunatic. So I was safe. Thank you," she said to me, holding out her hand.

I looked down at it, amused, and then looked up at her.

"Well, it was a huge inconvenience to have you in my car. Now it's just going to smell like whatever perfume you have on."

Kingston muttered something under his breath and I ignored him. I was rusty at this, sue me.

"Your car probably smells like I was just on a hike." Then she let out a little oof as Claire elbowed her in the side.

"She totally owes you. And, I have a perfect idea. She can take you out to dinner."

I looked at the soft-looking Claire, and at the flabbergasted look on Phoebe's face.

Oh, this was going to be interesting. I liked Claire. Though she didn't intrigue me as much as Phoebe.

"Claire," Phoebe muttered under her breath.

"You know, that sounds about right." I looked over at Kingston as he spoke, aware that I now had two people in my corner. This was a good day, bear and all.

"I don't need to put you out."

I held up my hands. "No, they're right. You should take me to dinner. And that way I can make sure you're really okay after the whole bear scare."

I practically felt Kingston's eyes roll to the back of his head as Claire beamed and Phoebe blushed.

"Dinner? Really?"

"Oh yes. Dinner."

And I was just going to have to find a certain black bear and thank him for this. Because this was one way to meet a woman, one I hadn't expected. And I sure as hell didn't mind.

Later that evening, I sat across the table from Phoebe and sipped from my water glass.

We had exchanged numbers at the top of the hill, and then decided what restaurant we would meet at. I didn't mind that Phoebe hadn't wanted me to pick her up. It was safer for her in any situation that we meet up at a neutral location. As someone who worked more stalker cases with ex-boyfriends than I cared to admit, I liked that she was being safe about this.

Kingston had given me shit over how I had gotten this date, but that was Kingston, constantly giving me shit about everything. I didn't mind though, because it just meant that I had gotten the girl, and Kingston hadn't.

Now Kingston was off working with Daisy, while I had a beautiful woman in front of me.

"You're an interior designer?" I asked, putting my brain back into the moment, and not over the fact that I was stressed that they were at physical therapy.

"Yes. I work for a company that was thankfully there for me during my internship when I was in college. I'm just grateful that it all worked out and they had a spot for me when I graduated."

I nodded, watching as her face lit up any time she talked about her job.

"I have no artistic talent when it comes to that. My

house that I share with Kingston looks like an actual bachelor pad."

"You live with your cousin?" she asked and then winced. "I mean, I live with Claire, so it's not like I can judge."

"Yes, we live together, though at this point I think it's just because we're used to it. We each own a part of our business, but we share it with a few more cousins, so it's not like we're rolling in business ties."

She smiled at that. "I like the fact that you work with your family. I do not, and I'm a little glad that I don't."

I scowled. "Do they treat you badly?"

Her eyes widened and she shook her head.

"No, the exact opposite. They're so caring. But I'm the baby sister. So they're constantly wanting to know what I am doing, and asking how they can help me. They wanted me to move back in with one of them after I got out of college so I could be under their care and not have to worry about rent or anything. But it's not like they're so much older than me that they have multiple homes or something for me to stay in. They just want to take care of me. I don't think they realize that I'm an actual adult."

"I have more cousins than I can count, and we're all pretty close, even the ones far younger. I have to say I'm one of the overprotective ones. Sorry."

She gave me a look, and then rolled her eyes. "You know, I'm not exactly surprised by that statement."

I laughed. "I feel like I should be offended at that, but I'm not. I'm an asshole when it comes to people hurting my family. And in my job sometimes I see the worst of the worst, so I'm an asshole all the time." I frowned. "Do you want me to stop cussing?"

She shook her head.

"No, I think my older sister can curse more than you."

My brows rose. "Well, that's good to know."

"She has to deal with men who ignore her or try to take advantage of her brain day in and day out. She can stand up to any one of them. I love her for it, and I want to be her when I grow up." Phoebe winced. "Here I am saying I'm an adult, and I say something like that."

"My parents use that phrase all the time. It's not a bad thing."

"You work in security?" she asked, frowning.

"I do. It's not as scary as it sounds." Or maybe it didn't sound scary enough. But I didn't say that. No need to scare her on our first date. I had enough trouble dating when it came to my job, and I did my best to downplay what I did. If I didn't, I either got women who only wanted danger—or at least they thought they did—or they ran away the first time I explained exactly what it was I did.

"So, do you install security systems, or are you like a bodyguard or something?"

"Most people think that it's either one or the other, not a mix."

"Well, I don't know. I just know security from movies."

I shook my head. "It's nothing like that. A lot of its research. I'm more on the bodyguard side of things, while my cousins do the installations more often than not, as well as the total recon setups. I do better on one-on-one."

Her eyes darkened as I said that, and I hadn't even meant to sound like I was flirting. Okay, that was a complete lie. I always wanted to sound like I was flirting when it came to her. Interesting.

As we continued to eat and talk, I fell more into being relaxed than I thought possible.

I liked this Phoebe. She was sexy, smart, and her sense of humor was top-notch. Plus, meeting her thanks to a black bear just seemed like a good story to tell about how we met.

The evening sped by, and before I knew it, I was walking her to her car door. I knew I wanted her, but maybe not the first night. I could see the hesitation in her gaze; it had been a long day after all.

So I pushed her hair back from her face, and cupped her cheek.

"Can I kiss you?" I asked.

Her eyes widened. "That line is directly from my favorite movie as a kid."

"Well, can I?" I asked, my voice a growl. Holding back was killing me but I'd never do anything to hurt her.

When she nodded, I pressed my lips to hers, softly at first, then a bit deeper.

Her hands went to my hips, gripping tightly, as I deepened the kiss, my tongue brushing along hers.

But we were in a parking lot, right under a light where anyone could see, so I leaned back and licked my lips. Her gaze followed the motion, and my cock pressed against my zipper.

"Can I take you out again?" I asked, my voice a growl.

"Oh. Yes. I'd like that."

I smiled, relieved and delighted.

I liked this Phoebe. This sweet woman who didn't have all the baggage that came with knowing the Montgomerys and our huge family. It wasn't that my family was a burden, but more like everybody seemed to know us, and sometimes it was nice to be with a woman who had no preconceptions about my family, my job, or who I was.

I kissed her again and squeezed her hand—I had a good feeling about this.

It was a promise. A beginning.

I hoped I didn't fuck it up.

Chapter Three

Kane

Now

It had been the week of all weeks, the year of all years. Not that I was ever going to say that out loud —that was just asking for more trouble. I wasn't usually one to believe in fate or luck, especially not with the year I'd been having, however maybe there was a way to get through the next few weeks. And forget that things kept getting in my way and making things even more difficult.

I still couldn't believe everything that had happened. Or that we still didn't have answers. I'd almost lost one of my best friends all because of someone's ego.

That was rich coming from me, because yes, we Montgomerys had egos. Though I wasn't a Montgomery by last name.

I had my dad's last name, and a big family without even adding in the Montgomerys. My aunts all had huge families, and my dad just happened to marry a Montgomery, so I had Montgomery as my middle name, just like many other cousins. I wasn't sure which of my aunts and uncles had decided to make that a thing, but apparently the Montgomery name would not die.

"What's going on?" Kingston asked from where he stood next to me, a frown on his face.

I shook my head.

"Nothing's wrong."

"That sounds like a lie," Kingston said with a laugh. We were the closest cousins in our business. Kingston and I were close in age, and though technically we were second cousins, two offshoots of the family tree, we acted more like brothers than anything. Which meant Kingston could read my mind when I didn't want him to. The damn man.

"So, you're not going to talk about it." Kingston paused. "Her?"

I whirled on him, narrowing my gaze. "No, we're not. You know we're not. You know *why* we're not."

"The thing is, I don't actually. I don't know why

you're acting this way. I don't know why you won't talk about her. Or that some really huge fucking things happened and you're not talking about them, either."

"What am I supposed to talk about? It didn't work out. Daisy's safe. Our family's safe. Our work is good. Business is up. What else is there? I don't want to talk about it. Okay?"

"If you didn't sound so defensive about it, maybe I would believe you."

"Maybe it's not for you to believe me. Just go. I'm going to close up shop and head out."

"You can talk to me, you know. You can talk to any of us. You don't have to keep it inside anymore."

I glared at him. "That's pretty rich coming from you."

Kingston shut up, his eyes going cold.

"You're an asshole sometimes, you know."

"Right back at you."

He huffed and grabbed his phone from his desk.

"Come to the bar with us. We should stop hiding shit."

"I'm fine. I promise."

Kingston gave me one last look before he headed out, locking the front door behind him. I'd go out the back way, ensuring everything was locked up tight, the security cameras were going, and set the alarm. We were all set to go.

So why did I have a tingle on the back of my neck?

Maybe because we still hadn't found one last guy. The cops were looking for him, but he was long gone. He'd taken his money and run off. We all knew that. But I still had an uneasy feeling.

I grabbed my things, did one last check around the building, and made my way out to the back parking lot where the employees parked. It was dark outside, but we had enough lights going so there were no shadows to hide in. Considering we not only owned the building, but each of the businesses inside were owned by our family, why the hell would we risk their safety? After all, we'd had enough happen to us recently, enough horror and terror, that we amped up our own security. It was our job to protect our family. And we had failed more often than not. But never again.

"Montgomery."

I froze at the familiar voice, even though it wasn't my name, and turned.

I knew that face, knew that voice, but hadn't expected to see it here.

"What do you think you're going to accomplish here?" I asked, my hands still in my pockets. I did my best to try to dial my phone without making it look like I was, but the man's gaze narrowed, his finger tightening on the trigger.

Fuck.

"Hands out of your fucking pockets."

I slowly did as he asked, cursing under my breath for letting Kingston go by himself. But at least he wasn't here for this. I'd talk my way out of this, just like I talked my way out of everything. But why hadn't we seen him coming? I looked up and saw the knocked-out security camera. Fuck. Well, the man was fast. And good.

But I was better.

"Let's just talk this out."

"Fuck you, Montgomery."

"Kane?" a soft voice asked and the blood in my veins froze, my entire body going on alert.

"Phoebe, get out of here!" I called.

The man turned towards her, whirling with the gun in his hand. I didn't think twice, I just moved, throwing myself towards Phoebe as her eyes widened at the sight of the man behind the dumpster, gun raised, and I knew fate was laughing at me for thinking it didn't exist.

Because it did. It always did.

She looked at me and I saw the confusion and terror in her gaze. I saw everything I hadn't been able to before.

Because she was the woman I loved. The woman that wasn't mine. I threw myself on top of her, and when the gun went off, she screamed.

By the time I pulled myself off her and looked up, the man with the gun was gone. The man we had been chasing for months. Months where we didn't realize that he was the one trying to sabotage the company. With bad calls, sabotaging our infrastructure, and doing what he could online and off to try to break us. And yet, all that went out the window. I'd find that man. That bastard. I didn't have another choice. But first I had to deal with the woman currently underneath me, eyes wide and hands shaking as she placed them on my chest.

"Kane? Oh my God. That man just shot at us. Are you okay?"

I loved this woman. And I hated that I did. Because every time I reminded myself that I loved her, I was also reminded about the fact that she wasn't mine. And she was never going to be mine. In that moment that didn't matter. All that did was the searing pain in my upper arm, and that I had no idea if the woman I loved was hurt or not.

"Are you okay?"

Her hands came away with blood and I cursed, sitting up as I ignored the fire scorching down my arm. Rage poured through me and my hands nearly shook. It took all of my training to calm myself and focus on the woman in my arms.

"Fuck. You're bleeding. You're hurt. Where are you hurt?"

There were pounding footsteps running towards us, and my head shot up, past her, on alert. But it was only Kingston, coming back.

"I'm not hurt. I mean, probably a little scraped from hitting the ground, but you're the one bleeding, Kane. You're shot."

Her hand went up to my arm and hovered over it, before she pulled her hands back.

"Am I supposed to put pressure on this? Oh my God. I don't know what I'm supposed to do. Your cousin's coming. He'll know what to do." She looked over her shoulder as Kingston came running, and I felt her stiffen when she realized that Kingston's gun was in his hand.

"I didn't see who ran off. Fuck. You're shot?" Kingston's gaze slid over mine, then down to Phoebe. "Phoebe? What are you doing here?"

"I..." She shook her head. "It doesn't matter. Kane's hurt. Should I put pressure on it? I mean, you guys know what to do in these situations. And I literally do not. Should I move him? Wait. Should we call the cops? We need to call the authorities."

She was rambling now.

Pushing away the pain in my arm, and from the scrapes and bruises from falling on the asphalt, I cupped her face, ignoring the sight of my own blood on her porcelain skin.

My blood was on her. Just like every fucking dream I had leading to our breakup. She was hurt, I could see the scrapes on her hands, the fear in her eyes. That was because she had come to me at my place of business and gotten hurt because of a man I couldn't fucking catch.

The blood on her skin was just a way too visual reminder of that.

"I'll be okay. I'm fine."

"Put pressure on it," Kingston said as he handed Phoebe a bandage.

I scowled up at him, but I saw the anger in his gaze over the fact that there were going to be questions. Kingston was fucking pissed. Just like I was, yet on a different spectrum. Because I was furious that Phoebe was hurt, while Kingston was pissed off because I was hurt. And we were both pissed over the fact that somebody had done this on our property. Again.

"Security's all up, Noah's on it. Cops are on the way, I'm sliding the gun away, but I have all my paperwork, so it's not going to be an issue."

I let out a string of curses as Phoebe pressed the bandage to my shoulder, her face paling.

"I'm hurting you. Damn it. I'm not good at this. I'm an interior decorator. Not a doctor."

"Nice *Star Trek* reference," Kingston said with a twitch of his lips, though the humor didn't reach his eyes. He was trying to calm her down—and probably me as well. I was ready to rip the door off the place and hide Phoebe inside before I chased down the asshole who dared hurt her.

I ignored the voice in my head telling me that *I'd* been the one to hurt her while trying to protect her. Yet another reason we weren't together.

Phoebe scowled at him. "Shouldn't we move him? What if the guy comes back?" Somehow she paled even further, and I cursed.

"You're going to be okay. I'm not going to let anyone hurt you."

"But they hurt you."

I wanted to hold her close, to reach out and press my lips to her forehead, but that wasn't my place. I didn't even know why she was here. Maybe to bring back my toothbrush, though I was sure we were well past that in our breakup. But she was here, and she had blood on her skin because of me.

By the time the authorities were there, and our cousins showed up, we thankfully weren't taken away and handcuffed over the fact that Kingston was armed. Instead we handed over our security footage as the authorities prowled the parking lot and building, and once again our family, teams, and everyone else that worked near us were inconvenienced because we had fucked up. Because we couldn't catch this damn man.

The owner of Sherman Priority Security. The one man we hadn't been able to get after the whole fucking fiasco.

Now I was sitting in a hospital bed in the ER, getting stitched up by a pretty doctor who kept scowling at me every time I moved.

"Mr. Carr, if you don't stop moving, you're going to scar."

I shrugged, making her scowl again even as the pain ricocheted through my shoulder. "I have more than a few scars."

"As I can see, since you're shirtless, and your line of work is congruent with this. However, you don't need a roadmap of your work history on your skin. So why don't you sit still while I do what I do best. Because I'm really damn good at this. But not if you keep moving."

Both of her nurses snorted, and I smiled. "That's good to know."

"I know one of your cousins, and an aunt, I think. And they taught me how to deal with you Montgomerys and your ilk."

I scowled, and then it all clicked. She had to be talking

about one of my aunts. Not my actual aunt by blood, but a cousin of a cousin in our family counted.

"The Gallaghers are worse."

"That's what you Montgomerys and Carrs say. Then again, you are the one currently in my place of business while I stitch you up."

I couldn't fault her there. I needed to get out. I needed to check on her. On Phoebe. Why had she shown up? And why couldn't I get her out of my head?

The doctor finished up and gave me home-care instructions. I nodded. "I've got it, I know the drill." All too well—and not something I'd let Phoebe hear.

"You're lucky it was an actual flesh wound. It didn't cut through any arteries or bone, but you did end up with quite a few stitches. I want you in that sling for at least two weeks."

"No way. I don't do slings."

"He'll wear the damn sling," Kingston said as he stormed into the room. "He'll wear it, and he will be happy about it. I'll even take a photo of it while he's smiling and send it to you."

The doctor just raised a brow. "Well, if that keeps him in a crappy mood, maybe he won't get shot again, so I'll take it."

"That requires me to get your number," Kingston said,

and the doctor just rolled her eyes before she left the room, one of her nurses laughing beside her.

"Did you seriously just hit on the woman that stitched me up?"

"Maybe. I'll get her number. It's always good to have them on call since our family keeps getting fucking hurt."

I nearly reached up to scrub my hand over my face and then realized that I was in the damn sling and everything hurt.

"Phoebe?"

"She's in a room a couple of doors down."

I tried to get off the bed, but Kingston put his hand on my good shoulder and glared. "Sit here while the rest show up so we can debrief. She's fine. A few scrapes from the asphalt, but you shielded her. Not only from the bullet, but from everything else. The only reason that she is still here is that all of her family is making sure she doesn't need anything else. If you thought we were over-protective, her family is trying to outdo us."

"Don't remind me," I grumbled.

Phoebe's siblings hadn't hated me, they just hadn't known what to do with me. Phoebe was the baby of their family, the youngest of four daughters and a son. Of course they hadn't wanted their baby sister to be with a "rough-and-tumble guy," in their words. They hadn't been mean about it, but they had been protective. And while I honored that, and agreed somewhat, I had resented it. Now though? They had been right. Phoebe had been in danger because of me. She had my blood on her hands and face because of me. Her family should have taken me out back and shot me or buried me in a deep hole so I couldn't ever hurt their precious baby sister. They had treated me with respect, made me feel welcome, but had always been protective. So I deserved any lashing that came my way once Isabella, Phoebe's oldest sister, figured out where I was.

"But she's okay?"

"Yes, she is," Ford said as he walked in, scowl in place. His partner in more ways than one, and my cousin, Noah, walked in, with a similar scowl.

And then Daisy, her boyfriend and coworker and our partner, Hugh, walked in as well.

"So it's the whole family," I grumbled.

"Pretty much," Daisy said, as she moved toward me, cupped my face, and pressed my forehead to hers. "Never do that again. That scared me."

"You're the one who got hurt recently. Why are you even here?"

"Like I can keep her away," Hugh grumbled, his familiar British accent not so calm like he usually was.

"You guys don't need to be here. You should be with your kid."

Hugh shook his head. "She's with Daisy's parents. And we're here because we want to know what the hell happened."

"Tim Sherman. He's the one who shot me."

"You saw his face?" Ford asked.

I scowled. "Yes. I saw his face, the shape of his body, and I saw him run away when he realized he didn't get his target."

"Hmm," Ford said, looking down at his phone.

"What? Don't you have the security footage?"

"We do. But his face wasn't on it."

"I saw him." I hadn't imagined the man who hated my family more than anything.

"You also had Phoebe there, and you had to make sure she was safe. Are you sure you saw him and not someone that maybe looked similar to him?" Daisy asked slowly, and I reeled back before I cursed under my breath.

"The cops have been looking for this guy for what he did to us and Daisy. Why do you think I'm seeing things?"

"Because the cops don't believe it was him. It could have been anyone that doesn't like what we do for a living. We've angered quite a few people by protecting those in need. And why was Phoebe there?" Noah asked, his voice steady—too steady.

I tried to bolt out of my bed, but Daisy pushed me back on my good shoulder.

"Rest for a minute. We're going to go talk with Phoebe."

"The fuck you are. I'm going to talk with Phoebe. I'm the one that got hurt."

"Don't put that on yourself," Kingston growled. "If anything, it's all of our faults."

"Or how about we blame the guy who actually shot you," Hugh said, ever the voice of reason. If he was going to join our family like I figured he would at any minute, he was going to have to panic with us. It helped.

"I need to talk to Phoebe. But we all know what that man wanted."

"To take out the Montgomerys," Noah said succinctly.

And it was true. Just because I didn't carry Montgomery as my last name, didn't make me not a Montgomery. It was my middle name, just like it was the middle name of all of my first cousins that happened to come from my dad's side of the family. I didn't know why they had done it, but I liked it. It gave me that sense of family. I had cousins and aunts and uncles and other family members that I loved on the Carr side, as well as everyone connected with them. But I also loved the crazy Montgomerys that I happened to be part of. So it didn't matter to me that I had a different last name because my mother was the Montgomery. She still held the Montgomery name as a middle name, just like I did. And we

Montgomerys stood together, in the face of adversity, terror, and apparently, a shooter.

"I need to talk with Phoebe."

"Okay. But let's go through it again. I know you already did this with the cops, and I do believe you, you know," Ford said, and I scowled at Kingston.

"You're the only one that doesn't believe me?"

My cousin sighed. "I didn't see his face. And I really want it to be anyone else."

"Why do you want the man who shot at me to be someone in addition to the person that already wants to kill us?" I asked.

"Because if it was anyone else, we could easily find him and this would be over. Now I just have a feeling it's going to get worse."

And on that, the floor fell out from under me and I just sat there, going over everything again, and knew this wasn't going to end well.

The authorities would find him—they had to. Because if they didn't? I was going to find him first. Because nobody was going to scare Phoebe. Not even me. I might not be able to claim her as mine, but part of me would always know she was my woman. And I would do anything to protect her. Even burn down the world and my reputation along the way.

Chapter Four

Phoebe

All I really wanted to do was close my door and pretend that none of this had happened. Only I didn't think I was going to have a choice, not when my family wouldn't leave me alone. I mean, I loved my family. I truly did. They were kind, generous, and always took care of me. Even if that meant they were overbearing to the point that they made me want to rip my hair out.

Case in point, I hadn't been shot. If anything, I had probably been in the way and was the reason Kane got hurt, more than he would have if I hadn't been there.

I hadn't been admitted to the hospital, and I hadn't even needed to go to the ER. But Kane and the others wouldn't consider anything else. So I had gone with him to the ER, and then hadn't been able to see him. Not only had my family pretty much forbidden it, Kane hadn't come to me.

I didn't know why that hurt me. We weren't together anymore, we both made sure of that. He wasn't mine to check on, nor was I his. I should just get that in my brain and forget that anything had happened. But I couldn't. I wanted to know more. I wanted to make sure he was safe. That he was being taken care of.

Who was going to tuck him in and make sure that he actually rested?

I had a few cuts and scrapes, my palms taking the brunt of it when I fell because Kane pushed me out of the way of a damn bullet. But I wasn't the one who'd been shot at. Not technically. He had, and had bled on me. And I hadn't been sure how to help him until Kingston arrived and told me what to do.

I hated feeling inept and like I wasn't smart enough to handle things on my own.

But that wasn't in my wheelhouse. This was in their wheelhouse. They dealt with things like this often. Kane put himself in danger and there was nothing I could do about it. There hadn't been anything I could do about it when we were together, and there sure as hell wasn't anything now that we were separated.

Annoyed with myself for my train of thought, I glared at my older sister.

I loved Isabella. She had shoulder-length dark hair with my eyes, sharp cheekbones, and a no-nonsense attitude that meant that she could get what she wanted out of anyone most days.

She'd had to.

She was the eldest of us and took that responsibility seriously.

Considering our father was rarely in our lives, she had been the one to take care of us.

Our mother mothered just as much as Isabella did. But with Dad constantly on work trips, and the two of them never actually married, Isabella had taken the bulk of the responsibility.

It didn't matter that I had two other older sisters and an older brother, Isabella had always taken the role of protector.

Our father sure as hell wouldn't have done it. No, he and my mother had loved each other, according to our mother, and had always done their best to make sure that we weren't caught in the middle of their dramatic love affair.

I was pretty sure my mom still loved my father, even though he was rarely around. He always showed up with huge promises, giant presents, and then left as if he had never been there, though the scars of his manic happiness always left evidence.

My mother loved him, even though he was a wild-child with a life of his own.

I hated that I was even thinking about him right now.

I wasn't sure if Isabella had called Dad to tell him that I was hurt.

I sure as hell hoped not.

"Isabella, I'm fine. Go annoy someone else."

My eldest sister scowled at me. "You're lucky I don't tuck you in so tightly that you're unable to move, missy. Why were you at the Montgomerys? What on earth do you need from your ex?"

"Stop badgering her," Sophia, the second oldest of us, said as she came forward, a tray in hand.

"I'm not badgering, I'm asking."

"More like interrogating," Kyler grumbled as he walked into my bedroom and flopped into the armchair in the corner. More like draped himself. He somehow made it look effortless, his hair falling over his forehead in a dramatic way, and I just rolled my eyes at him.

Kyler was an "artist"—he had the temperament of an artist sometimes. But the way he had one leg propped up over the arm of the chair, and his beautifully sculpted cheekbones resting on his fist, he looked like he was ready for a cover shoot for Rolling Stone.

And yet, he would fight to the end of the earth for his siblings, and both of our parents. Because for some reason he and Dad still got along. I'm not quite sure why.

"I know Emily is out of town, but why are you guys all here?" I asked. I let Sophia settle me against the headboard with fluffy pillows behind me. I looked down at the tea and toast in front of me, with perfect marmalade jam, and narrowed my gaze at my beautiful sister.

Sophia was tall and elegant, a former principal dancer for the Denver Ballet. She had retired a year ago, not because she couldn't out dance anyone there, but because she wanted to start a new phase of life while she could still enjoy it. Now she was a dance teacher and working on starting her own dance studio. I couldn't sometimes believe that my elegant and beautiful sister, who had put her body through the wringer in order to become a principal dancer, was somehow related to me. I was far shorter, far rounder, and had significantly worse coordination and balance.

As was evidenced by the fact that they had put me in bed immediately, as if I were a Victorian child with a cough, when all I had done was fall.

"Seriously, why were you there?" Isabella asked, and I ran my hand over my face.

I wasn't going to tell them. They didn't have a right to know. No, that was a lie, they had every right to know, but I couldn't let them know. Not when I knew as soon as I said the words, I would worry them to the point that the current mothering and hovering was going to pale in comparison to how they would act if they knew. I needed to talk to someone who actually knew what they were doing, hence why I needed to talk to Kane. Only I wasn't sure how to get to him if he wasn't going to let me see him.

I needed to stop acting so irrational when it came to him. But that was always my problem.

"It doesn't matter why I was there. It's Kane. I don't know why it's any of your business." I didn't mean to sound so rude, and from the way that my siblings looked at me, they knew it was out of character.

"I'm sure you feel that way, as you tell us that often." Isabella's tone turned icy, and I winced.

"I'm sorry."

"Don't be sorry," Sophia said as she patted my cheek. "You're hurt, and you're grouchy. And Isabella is grouchier."

"Just like a cat when someone steps on its tail," Kyler grumbled while Isabella scowled. I flipped him off. He smiled that beautiful smile of his, the one that made every single person around us fall at his feet since we were toddlers. "There she is. My loving sister."

"I'm really okay. I'm not even hurt."

"You were in the *hospital*," Isabella added.

"Because it was an overreaction. Kane was the one

that was hurt." I swallowed hard, the sight of his blood still unnerving me.

"That's why you shouldn't be with him anymore. He works a dangerous job and you got hurt because of it."

I ignored the guilt because I wasn't sure that was true. I'd gone to him for a reason. "He protects people."

"He didn't protect you," Isabella snapped. We butted heads more often than not because Isabella wanted to keep me safe—just like she did the rest of the family. And she got angry when she didn't have control over a situation.

Sophia stood between us, arms outstretched. "Stop it. Isabella, you liked Kane, don't act like you suddenly hate him. He does good work, and he did the security for this apartment and your house. Why are you acting like this?"

"Yes, why are you?" another voice said as my roommate and best friend walked in. "Thank you all for letting me know that my best friend and roommate was hurt, by the way," Claire grumbled.

"Damn it, I'm sorry," Isabella said, pinching the bridge of her nose. "We're gearing up for tax season, and I fucked up. My brain's doing too many things."

Claire reached out and gave Isabella a one-armed hug.

"It's okay. But seriously, next time that my best friend gets shot at, maybe let me know."

"I'm fine. Have you heard from Kane?" I asked.

Claire shook her head. "No, I only heard because Kingston mentioned it."

I raised a brow and she waved me off. "Group chat. You're part of it too, so I'm sure you got the text."

I glared at Kyler, who had the grace to look a little embarrassed as he pulled my phone out of his pocket. "I didn't read any of the texts. I was just making sure you got some rest."

"How is all of you in here hovering over me when I'm not even hurt helping me rest?" I asked as I put my hand out for my phone.

He slid off the armchair in a smooth and fluid move, one that I saw Claire notice. Claire had always had a crush on Kyler, not that she would do anything about it, and I'm pretty sure Kyler would never do anything about it either. Or maybe they had and they weren't going to tell me. It didn't matter though because I had a feeling Claire was meant for someone else. Of course, my thoughts on that meant nothing because I thought I was meant for Kane, but here we were.

"Thank you for my phone, now everybody get out. You've fed me, overprotected me, and now I'm in bed when I'm really fine. I could run a mile right now."

Claire blinked at me.

"Okay, I could walk a mile very quickly," I corrected, and all three of my siblings laughed.

"We'll leave you be, and I'll update Emily too," Sophia said as she tugged Kyler and Isabella out of the room.

"Be safe, lock the doors, and give us any updates you have from the authorities, okay?" she added, and then put her hand over Isabella's mouth as she literally dragged my eldest sister out. Kyler laughed, closing the door behind him, leaving Claire and me alone.

"So, you really okay?" Claire asked, and I heard the honest worry underneath her tone.

I nodded, rubbing a hand over my chest.

"I'm fine. Really. Kane's the one who got hurt."

"Do you want me to ask Kingston if he's okay?"

I shook my head. "No, it's fine."

"That sounded like a lie," she grumbled.

"I know you have work to do, so go do it and I'll just sit here and wallow in my own self-pity."

"Why were you there, Phoebe?"

"No reason," I lied. I needed to tell her. She deserved to know because she could be in danger too. I hated keeping secrets from my best friend and from my family. But maybe I was just overreacting. That's why I needed to talk to Kane. Why I had been there in the first place. And yet it all felt as if it was too much.

"I'd like to know why you were there too," a deep voice said from the now open door. I hadn't even realized the door had opened at all, and from the way Claire gasped and whirled, I realized she hadn't either.

"You scared the hell out of me," she snapped before her shoulders relaxed.

I did the same, my heart aching. He had a sling on his arm and looked so pale. He had been shot in front of me, and now here he was, standing in my room as if he were fine, while I was lying down like an invalid.

"What are you doing out of the hospital?" I blurted.

"I'm fine. Seriously. I'm fucking fine," he grumbled as he slid the sling off his arm. I didn't miss the wince that he tried to hide as he tossed the sling down to the armchair.

Claire looked between us and held up her hands.

"You know, I don't need to be a part of this. But I will get details later, okay? Because you're hiding something, and you don't hide things from your best friend," Claire said as she glared at me, then looked up at Kane. "Don't hurt her."

Kane's eyes darkened at the warning, but he nodded briskly. "I don't have any plans to."

"We never do," she whispered before she left the room, closing the door behind her. I knew it was the strength of her character that allowed her to leave with so much curiosity in her gaze. I wasn't sure I would've been able to do the same if the shoe were on the other foot.

Alarm shot through me as I put the tray to the side and scrambled out of bed.

"Get back in bed."

"No, you should. You're the one who needs to be in bed."

He raised a brow. "You're asking me to your bed?"

I let out a small growl, throwing my hands up in the air. "Are you serious right now?"

He sighed and ran his hand over his face, wincing as it jostled his shoulder.

"I'm fine. It was a graze, and I have stitches. I hate the sling. It hurts my neck more than anything."

"Let's just sit down then. You got shot tonight."

"And you got thrown to the ground."

"I just have a few cuts on my hands. See." I held up my hands, and I realized it was the wrong thing to do when his eyes darkened.

"You got hurt because of me," he growled, his voice low and pained.

I moved forward before I even realized I was doing it. I put my hand on his chest, ignoring the slight sting from the cuts. I could feel his heartbeat underneath my palms, that familiar rhythm that always helped me sleep. Because I had known he was there. Always.

Of course, that had been one of the problems.

"You got hurt because of me," he whispered again, his gaze on mine.

I swallowed. "No, it could have been because of me." There, I said the words; I broached the subject. Because there *was* a reason I had gone to his place. I had needed help.

"What are you talking about?" he asked, his whole body stiffening.

I'd made a mistake. More than one. I shouldn't have gone to him for this. I should have gone to Kingston, or anyone else. Another company for that matter. Maybe I was just overreacting, and I hadn't needed anyone at all, but I shouldn't have gone to Kane. All it did was bring back old hurts.

"Never mind," I whispered and turned away. He reached out and gripped my wrists before I could get very far.

"Phoebe, what the hell?"

"It's fine. It's really fine."

"No, it's not. The shooter was someone after our team. Someone that hurt Daisy and Kingston."

My eyes widened, remembering when they were hurt.

"Are they okay? Oh my God, did they get hurt again?"

Kane swallowed hard. "Everyone's fine. Or they will be. But do you remember Tim Sherman?"

I nodded. "He owned that security company that was your rival."

"'Was' being the operative word. Most of what's left of the company are in jail or having their business being dismantled. It's a whole shit show. But Tim is still out there. And he has a grudge."

I licked my lips, fear pulsing through me. "And he wants to hurt you? Who protects you?"

His lips twitched. "My family does. And I'm decent at doing it myself. At least when my head's on right."

"Then you should go. And make sure you're safe, I'll talk to someone else."

His eyes narrowed. "Wrong thing to say, sweet."

"Kane."

"Talk to me."

"I think I have a stalker," I blurted.

He blinked and then his jaw set, his hand fisting at his sides. "What?"

"I might be wrong. But I've gotten a few letters and a few phone calls where all I can hear is breathing on the line. And I can't figure out who is calling because they're from blocked numbers. I thought it was just spam at first, but now I don't know. It's just weird, and sometimes I feel like someone's watching me. Maybe I'm overreacting, and watching too many thriller movies and listening to those podcasts to get me to sleep at night."

"You still listen to those?"

"I like true crime stories where they talk peacefully and respectfully about the victim and their families, and when the families are involved. I can't help it."

"Tell me everything."

I shook my head. "No. I'll talk to someone else. I just realized that this is a horrible mistake."

Because I couldn't be the reason he got hurt again. And I wasn't sure I could even be in the same room with him. Not that I hated him. No, it was the exact opposite.

He was suddenly in my space, a hand on my waist. He always did that to keep me steady. Either that or cupped my cheek. He was always touching me, protecting me.

"Phoebe. What the hell?"

"I don't know. I think I'm overreacting."

He shook his head. "You don't overreact to things like that. Tell me everything."

I laid out the letters and described the phone calls. When I moved away to go to my desk, he glared at me. "I'm just getting to my journal. I made a note about the dates and details so I would remember. I thought I was losing my mind and overreacting."

When he looked through the list, his eyes went stormy and he glared at me. "There are seven calls on here, Phoebe."

"And they could have been spam. Maybe a tele-marketer."

"You obviously didn't think so if you made a list."

"I don't know what to do."

"Did you go to the authorities?"

I shook my head. "What are they going to do? Tell me that I'm crazy?"

"Then you'll have a paper trail."

I winced. "But there's no evidence."

"You have notes."

"That aren't addressed to me and were delivered to my place of business. They could be for anyone."

And that was the problem. It sounded as if I was over-reacting. I watched too many scary movies and had dated a man who helped protect people. I was probably more paranoid than most.

"Okay. We're going to figure it out. And I'm not leaving your side."

That was the exact opposite thing I needed him to say. Because while my heart leapt at the thought, my brain knew I needed to take a few steps back. Full stop and run away.

"I need someone else. It can't be you. I can pay, I promise. But it has to be someone else. For obvious reasons."

"You're not fucking paying, and no, you're getting me. I'm going to protect you."

And with that promise, I knew my fate had been sealed. Now Kane knew and there would be no getting away from this.

He was already hurt, and I could still feel his blood on my skin.

I refused to go through that again.

Chapter Five

Phoebe

I stood in my office, Kane at my side, wondering how I had gotten into this situation. I got myself here because I asked him to be here, so why was I even fretting? After all, I only had myself to blame.

Only it was difficult to focus on the patterns in front of me, as well as the spreadsheets on my screen, when I could feel him standing next to me. Lurking, all hot and bodyguard like.

I hated that I called him hot first. Because he was way more than just his good looks.

But oh my God, talk about good looks. No, he was more. Of course the man was more.

He was smart, caring, selfless. He always put everyone else before him, including his family, friends, and who he was seeing. In other words, he put himself last, and always made sure that whoever he was spending time with, whether it was family or someone he was dating, had their needs met.

Though he ignored the fact that sometimes I just wanted to do things for myself. For example, I turned to him as he held out my cup of coffee without a word. The man didn't even say anything. Didn't even ask if I wanted coffee. No, he just saw that I had finished my cup, and allowed myself a second cup an hour after I finished the first as long as I had water. And of course the damn man had made sure I had water as well.

Because of course he was seeing to my needs without me asking. He was just always there, watching, waiting, making sure I was always taken care of and never had to want for anything.

The damn man was insane.

No, *I* was insane.

Thank God he couldn't actually hear my thoughts, even though sometimes I thought he could. Because if he could, he'd think I'd lost my damn mind.

"Thank you," I said through gritted teeth, and tried not to be resentful of the fact that the man just wanted to keep me safe. I had hired him to do so, not that he actually let me pay him. He was doing this for me because I was his friend.

Dear God, I hated that word. Friend. We had been so

much more to each other—of course, it was my fault that we weren't anything more now, but I wasn't going to think about the details. Not when he was just always there, hovering. Doing what he did best and taking care of me.

I hated him.

But I still loved him.

And that was why this was not going to work.

"This isn't going to work."

"I have no idea what you're talking about," he said so calmly, so coolly, that I knew he knew exactly what I was talking about.

Damn the man.

"You're just always there. No matter what I do, you're there. And so helpful."

He raised a brow at me.

"Would you rather I not be helpful?"

"I would rather you not be here at all," I said, and then immediately regretted the words when I saw that flash of pain. Whether he meant for me to see it or not, I still saw it all too well. I had ended our relationship. Yes, for our own good, but wasn't that just the worst fucking thing to even think.

We weren't together because I had needed to breathe. Because he had needed to do the same even though he hadn't realized it. And he looked better for it.

Before he could say anything though, I reached out

and gripped his forearm. I knew it was a mistake as soon as I had but there was no going back now. I felt the heat from him on my skin and swallowed hard. It took everything within me not to lick my lips and meet his gaze. Instead, I let out a breath and let my hand fall.

"I'm sorry. That was uncalled for."

I wasn't sure what I was expecting him to say, but him leaning forward and taking my hand was not part of it. "I get you. You don't want me here because of why I'm here. But Noah and the team are working on it, Kingston's going through the information you gave him and the authorities, and we'll handle it. And since I am not allowed to be on too many active-duty things right now, thanks to nurses Noah and Ford," I snorted and grinned, just like he wanted me to, "I'm going to hang out with you."

"I see you're still not wearing your sling."

He looked like he was about to shrug and then thought better of it. "When it's in the sling, it hurts just as much as it does when it's not. I'm not planning on doing any heavy lifting or rolling around on the ground. Don't worry. I'm fine."

"You keep saying that, and yet I'm not quite sure I believe you. Do you know what fine means?"

He grinned. "Freaked out, insecure, neurotic, and emotional? No. Not so much."

"Is that a real thing? Or is that just from that movie with Charlize Theron?"

"I love how of all the people in that movie, you went with her. Not that I'm saying that's wrong."

"She was the hottest, and the most talented, and has the most Oscar nominations. I think. Well now, I have to go do the math on that because I might be wrong." I rolled my eyes and looked back at my desk. "You really don't have to sit in here and watch me do this. There were a couple of letters and phone calls. It's not like whoever is bothering me is at my house or in my office."

"But he was sending the notes to your office. Until we figure it out, I'm here."

"When you could be at home resting."

"We both know I don't rest."

"Okay, then go sit over there. You're hovering."

He shook his head. "I don't hover."

"You are the definition of hovering. I swear if I put you and Isabella in a room, all you would do is try to out-hover each other and then I would be locked in a box somewhere trying to figure out how to get unhovered."

"First off, unhovered isn't a word."

"Let me make a word up. I'm having a little bit of a panic episode."

"You're not having a panic episode. And second,

Isabella and I cannot be in a room together. We fight more often than not."

"Because you guys are the same person." I hadn't even realized that fact or that I was going to say it until I did and then I burst out laughing. "Oh my God. I was dating my older sister. I need to go to therapy. So much therapy."

Kane looked appalled until his lips twitched. "You were not dating your sister. I promise you, Isabella and I are not the same person."

"I don't know. You guys overwork yourselves, ignore injuries and illnesses, do your best to make sure you're the most amazing at your work, and you like to make sure that I never strain myself or make a misstep in any way."

"What on earth are you talking about?"

I shook my head and was thankful that my phone rang so I didn't have to figure out how exactly to explain myself to him.

"Jefferson Interior Designs, this is Phoebe speaking. How may I help you?"

I took notes as a potential client gave me their information and put more information into my spreadsheets.

"No problem. I can be out there next week, does Thursday at 8:oo a.m. work? Or is that too early? You're right. No, Mr. Jefferson doesn't have any space for the next year, but I'm fully certified and can fix all of this. You've seen my portfolio?" I nodded even though they couldn't see me. "Great. Let's go over a few more details."

As I wrapped up the phone call, and then the next, I didn't have any time to worry about Kane or the fact that he finally stopped hovering completely. I had work to do, orders to fulfill, and tomorrow I would be out at clients' houses, doing what I did best.

I was an interior designer and I loved what I did. I loved brightening up a house to be filled with memories, or have an office be functional and yet warm. I loved moody interiors and bright spots of color. I didn't like to gray wash, or monochrome anything. Thankfully, the person that I worked for was on the same page, and we didn't go crazy on the budget. We were moderately priced, which meant my commissions weren't as high as some of my fellow graduates, but I could pay my rent, at least with Claire as my roommate, and I had a small savings account. I counted that as a win.

Of course, with my long hours and Kane's, it meant that when we had been together, we hadn't seen each other enough. If I wasn't at a client's house, he was doing one of the countless things he had to do for his work. He worked all hours and sometimes he could set his own, since he was one of the co-owners of the company, but he couldn't take all the time off when he wanted to. We both put our careers before our relationship, and that was just one other thing that stood in the way of us. Just the thought of me dating again made me want to be sick, because I wasn't ready for that, but even if that did come up, I wasn't sure when I was going to find the time.

I barely had time with Claire these days, let alone my family. There was no time for men in my life.

I still wasn't sure how I had fit Kane in when we dated.

And then that made me think about what would happen when he was ready to fit another woman into his life. A woman that wouldn't be me. My hand tightened around my phone for an instant, before I focused back on the hold music. I did not need to think about Kane with anyone else. He could be with someone right now and I wouldn't know. I wouldn't have the right to know. We were no longer together. He was helping me as what? A friend? A client? An acquaintance he used to sleep with?

That thought made my saliva turn to sawdust and I swallowed hard, reaching for my water bottle.

He was going to find someone. Someone that he fit with and who wouldn't run away when things got tough. And he wouldn't feel as if he needed to protect them. He would find someone strong and capable that could handle things on their own. Someone who wouldn't come running to him over a few phone calls that were probably nothing.

I was overreacting. I still hadn't even told Claire or my siblings about it. Was this just a way for me to reach out to Kane? A horrible, sick way of wanting him in my life without having to have him in my life? To crawl back without asking for forgiveness.

Even if I didn't think I needed forgiveness?

The phone dropped its call and I glared at it.

"You okay over there?" he asked, his attention on his phone. I knew he was working over there since he had brought his tablet, but I wasn't sure what he was working on.

"I was on hold with the distributor, well, a potential distributor, and the call just dropped me. For the second time. I think I'm going to go with someone else."

"I hate customer service."

"It's usually not the other person's fault either. They're overworked, and you have to go through fifteen AI menus before you get to a real person."

"And then the mom-and-pop shops are either over-worked or don't know how to deal with phone calls or websites."

"Even in this day and age. It's exhausting."

"When do you get off work?"

"I don't have to go to a client's house today, so I can go home after that phone call." I had a few meetings earlier that day, that were easier to have at my office rather than at home since Claire had been working at home for the morning. While we could usually work together in the same apartment, having Kane there would've raised questions that I didn't have answers for.

And that reminded me I needed to do the one thing I should have to begin with.

"You know what? I was completely overreacting to this. I don't need your help. But I want to thank you for helping me with my delusions. Or at least calming me down. Nothing happened today, so I'm not going to waste any more of your time. You can go back to work. As long as you promise not to hurt yourself in the process."

Because he had still been shot. That person was still out there, and it made my palms sweat to even think about. I wanted to wrap him in cotton wool and keep him safe. But there was no way I could ever do that to Kane. I couldn't get him to stop doing that to me. How was I supposed to protect him? The answer: I wasn't.

I never got to protect Kane Montgomery Carr. He only got to protect me.

And the imbalance of that relationship and situation meant I'd had to walk away. I wasn't going to keep him in my life with a slight tether over something I was clearly overreacting about.

Kane raised a brow and turned his tablet towards me.

"You got another letter today. This one has a little

more detail. You want to tell me that you're overreacting now?"

Ice laced his words, and I went to him, my eyes widened.

"I got a letter? I didn't know."

"You were on the phone; it came at the top of your mail. Without a postmark. Meaning whoever did it left it here. I've already contacted the officer with your case, and they came by for it."

"Are you kidding me? What did it say? And why didn't you tell me?"

"The officer's going to talk to you tonight. I told him you were on a business call, and since he knows me, he'll deal with it later."

"What did it say?"

"You can read it here."

I see you. I'm sorry I scared you. But you're safe.

I promise you're safe.

I just want you to know that I will always be there to protect you.

I will always be there to watch over you.

To make sure that the others don't know.

You were always so caring. So attentive.

I see that. I understand. And don't worry.

I'll keep watching.

My mouth went dry, my hand shaking as I re-read the

letter once, twice.

"They've never been that long before."

"And the words changed to more possessive. The pronouns changed as well. A lot more I's. And you's. I'm not walking away from this. You worked your ass off today, and you finally looked a little more relaxed as the day went on. I wasn't going to change that."

"But this person is watching me."

"They are. And I'm going to figure out who the fuck it is."

"Kane," I began, and he shook his head.

"Come on. Let's get you out of here and talking to the person on your case, and then we'll go get you some dinner and take you home."

"This can't be right. They're just silly notes."

"I deal with silly notes all the time. And I'm going to make sure that whoever wrote this doesn't get near you."

I couldn't process what he was saying as I went on autopilot to gather my things. Speaking with the officer in charge went quickly, because they didn't have anything to add. It helped that Kane knew the man, and they had worked together in the past. I felt two steps behind, coming to terms with nothing making sense.

I just wanted this to end. I had been ready to kick him out of my office, to pretend that nothing like this had happened at all, but it was all too real.

We stopped by a little Greek place to pick up take out, and I hadn't even realized what we were doing until we were on the road.

"Wait, what? This isn't the way to my house."

"We're going to my place. I figured we should talk."

"Well, that doesn't sound foreboding at all."

"You were freaked out back there, and I don't think you've really processed it. Kingston's finishing up the security on your place, too," he added, and I nodded, finally understanding.

"And you're feeling just as weird as me?"

"Why would I feel weird?"

"Because you're having to watch me. I just, maybe Kingston should be here? Or maybe I don't need a body-guard. Maybe this can just all go away."

"First off, Kingston's not going to be watching you. That's on me. And after that note, you do. At least until we figure out what's going on. Noah and Ford aren't letting me out into the field beyond this anyway, so just know that I'm here because I want to be."

"And this isn't weird for you? That you're watching me? That we're in the same car together? Any of it?"

"I love watching you, Phoebe," he whispered as he glanced at me, and then his gaze was on the road again.

"What do you mean?"

"You're the best at what you do. I love your creativity.

You can fix any room on a budget or with a million dollars. Hell, my house is fucking amazing because of you."

I didn't even realize I was blushing until I felt the heat rush to my cheeks.

"Really?"

"Yes, really. I've always admired you and thought you were talented. And I like hanging out with you, even when it's because I'm protecting you."

I pressed my lips together, reality crashing in once again.

"Ah. That."

Because that was why we had broken up. I was the baby of the family and my siblings were all so overprotective sometimes, it was hard to breathe.

Kane was the same.

He wasn't a bully ex, no, he got growly and I felt stifled.

Maybe that was an issue that came from being abandoned by my father, but no, that just all circled back to the fact that I wasn't equal in this relationship.

And I wasn't ever going to be.

Someone was playing a game with me, scaring me, and yet here I was, running and asking Kane for help once again. This time it wasn't a bear, and Kane wasn't a stranger.

But I was still the damsel in distress.

And that was something I never wanted to be.
Especially with him.

Chapter Six

Kane

As soon as we were at a stoplight, I looked over at her, her silence digging in.

"What did I say?" I asked.

She didn't say anything, just sat and looked at her hands, her mind going in a million directions. I could always tell when it did from the way she pressed her thumbs together, her forehead scrunched as she tried to organize her thoughts. She constantly had a multitude of thoughts and imaginings going in that brain of hers. It was how she could take a simple room with four white walls and a lowered ceiling and somehow turn it into a warm masterpiece that fit the client perfectly. She was able to do all that in that mind of hers, all while having a full conversation with you without you realizing part of her brain was working on something else. I had always admired her for that, for her strength, her brilliance, and her beauty. We had met in a situation where she had been running for her life, and yet it turned into one of the most hilarious and serendipitous parts of my life.

"Come on, we're near my house. We're going to talk this through." Not only was someone stalking her, sending her threatening notes, calling her, there was something else going on. And we needed to get to the bottom of it.

"Kane. I'm fine. Really. We don't need to talk it out."

I shook my head as I went through the green light, taking the next street to my house. "Phoebe. We never talked about it."

"Kane."

"I want to know." I huffed. "I think we both deserve to know."

"Fine." Her voice was so small and I hated myself. But if this was the only way to get her in the same room with me where I wasn't going to growl or feel as if I was losing my damn mind, then I would take it. Because I fucking loved her and she had broken my heart. But maybe I'd just let her heart slip through my fingers. Maybe I hadn't tried hard enough. I had let her walk away and hadn't asked why. Maybe I just hadn't seen it all along and this was all on me. I wouldn't be fucking surprised. But I needed to figure it out. And frankly, we just needed to talk.

We went to my place and I quickly re-upped the security system, doing a walkthrough of the place. I had the best security system out there for my place. It helped that my family owned the company and ran it. And soon Phoebe was going to have the same exact system on her apartment with Claire. Kingston was texting me updates as he and Gus worked on it. I wanted to think that the safest place Phoebe could be was with me, but I knew that was a lie. After all, I still had a stitched-up wound on my arm, that I really should put back in that fucking sling, to show how wrong I was. If she had been safe with me, she wouldn't have been pushed to the ground when I tried to protect her because someone had been shooting at us.

"Can I get you something to drink?"

"I'm fine. We have dinner to eat, and I like my kabobs."

"At least get water. You don't want a beer or some wine?"

"You don't drink wine."

"I do sometimes." I paused. "I have a bottle of that pinot grigio that you like." I didn't look at her as I said it. But the fact that I had it, and I drank some of it whenever I wanted to think about her? That led me into pathetic territory. And I wasn't about to lead her down that path. I was already pathetic enough.

"Oh. Okay. Are you allowed to have beer or wine with your wound?"

I looked over my shoulder. "I'm not taking any pain meds for it. I'll have a beer. Or maybe I'll have that glass of wine. It's pretty good."

Her brows rose. "You never told me that when we were together."

"I'm afraid I didn't say a lot of things I should have when we were together."

She opened her mouth to say something, but I turned away to pour us two glasses of wine, as well as two glasses of water. She went through my kitchen as if she had never left, and the fact that she had just made it hurt more. She pulled out two plates, two sets of silverware, and set the small kitchen table as we pulled out the food from the bag and set out the containers.

"This is a lot of food," she commented.

I shrugged. "Leftovers are good, and Kingston can always have some."

"I like that he lives right next door to you."

"Yeah, it's good to have family close."

"And I bet they don't hover like my family does."

I looked at her, then threw my head back and laughed. "You dated me for how long? You know the Carrs and the Montgomerys are ridiculous when it comes to overprotectiveness and hovering. It's in the blood. The DNA. And those who are adopted in sort of assimilate into the culture. It's just what we do."

She met my gaze, something flashing over her eyes that I couldn't read.

When had I stopped being able to read her?

How many mistakes had we made?

We ate in silence for a few moments, but it wasn't awkward. It felt like we were falling back into rhythm. After a few bites I set my fork down, suddenly not hungry.

"Why did we break up, Phoebe?"

She stared at me for a moment before looking down at her hands and sighing. "We wanted different things," she finally said, and I shook my head at that familiar refrain.

"What things?" I asked, my voice steady. "We wanted each other. That sounds like the same damn thing to me. What did I do, Phoebe?"

She looked up at me then, her eyes wide with shock. "You didn't do anything."

"Just say the words. You don't have to be afraid of me. You're not fucking afraid of me, are you?"

Fear slid along my spine before she stood up quickly and came to my side, grabbing my hand.

"I've never been afraid of you. Maybe afraid of what you were making me feel, but that's just natural, isn't it?"

"I don't know, Phoebe. I never felt like this with anyone else."

"And yet..."

"And yet. We wanted each other. It looks like you still want me. I still want you. Why aren't we together?"

"Because you were just like my dad!" she blurted.

I blinked, so fucking confused. I had never met her father. It had always been an oversight in my opinion, but the man was rarely around. He had never married Phoebe's mother, but they acted like a nuclear family. But I knew the man was a bastard. Overprotective, growly, and it made my skin crawl to be compared to him.

"Excuse me?" I asked, shocked.

"Not in the horrible ways that he can be. But he was always so overprotective and growly and didn't let me go out or do what I wanted. At least when he was around. Most of the time he was working or dealing with life shit that wasn't our family, but when he was around he was always in our business. So controlling."

I stood up, moving so fast the chair fell behind me. "I'm...I'm controlling?" My mouth went dry and I looked back over every moment we had been together. Yes, I had wanted to make sure that Phoebe was safe, that my work never interfered with her day-to-day life. But controlling? "I'm that way with work, but I was never with you."

"Not in that way." She put her hands up, and then sighed, her eyes filling with tears. "Never in that way. I'm not using the right words."

"Then use better words, Phoebe. Why did we break

up? Am I that much of an asshole that you were afraid of me?"

If she said yes then I would call Kingston over here to take her home, and then I would stay out of her life. Because I had no clue that I was that kind of asshole. No fucking clue.

"No. I'm not saying this right. You always needed to make sure that your job never touched me."

"But it did. It fucking did."

"And that's not your fault. Everything you did put me in this little box. You tried to make sure that nothing bad ever happened to me, and I couldn't figure out how to say what I wanted. I didn't even know *what* I wanted. We just moved so fast, Kane. One day we were running from a bear."

I put up my hand, my mouth twitching. "Phoebe. Seriously?"

"No, one day we were running from a bear, and then I was practically at your house every night and barely seeing Claire and everything was just so serious and you always wanted to make sure I was safe and asking where I was when I wasn't with you. And it wasn't like I felt I always had to be with you. But you were always so afraid that something was going to happen to me. And I realized that with your job you're always worried that something's going to happen, but you were so afraid that you would hold me so tightly in your sleep that I would have to hold your cheek just so you could relax."

I swallowed, remembering the nightmares of her being run off the road, or someone kidnapping her. Of the thousand things that I saw on a daily basis with my job.

"I didn't realize that I hurt you."

"Never physically, and not even emotionally. You were just so worried that something would happen to me you couldn't see past that. And I know it was because of your job, and the fact that I have a fucking stalker now just reinforces that for you. You're standing by my side when you're obviously hurt because you're afraid something's going to happen."

"Because something *could* happen. You have a damn stalker who is sending you notes."

"I know, and it scares the hell out of me, but even before that you were always so worried that something was going to happen to me that you never were able to relax. You're always tense, always afraid. We met in a moment of high adrenaline, but even then you were far more relaxed. What happened?"

"Daisy was hurt. She got fucking blown up, and Kingston was hurt right alongside her. My family keeps getting hurt on their jobs and even when they don't have anything to do with security. I can't let that happen to you."

"But it wasn't going to. Or if it did, then it wouldn't have been your fault. Everything was just so much at the moment, and I was trying to get a promotion at my first job and I failed. Do you remember that?"

I shook my head. "You didn't fail, they went with the other person, the one sleeping with the boss."

"Yes, he was sleeping with the boss and doing a very good job of it, so I started over again on my own with Jefferson and it was all too much. I just felt stifled. Like I was suffocating in my own stress, and then you were doing the same and neither one of us were breathing. Not only was I feeling like I couldn't get out, you were stuck in the same position. Always worried about what was going to happen to Leif or Kingston or Lake. Your family kept getting hurt and yet you were so afraid that I was going to also. You weren't even thinking about yourself. It wasn't healthy, Kane. So no, you weren't controlling. That was the worst word to use. But you were so scared that you put us both in these boxes that we couldn't escape from. And I didn't want you to hate yourself if I got hurt. Just like I know you're beating yourself up now even though you threw your body on top of mine. You protected me. So I know there're still feelings and there's still something between us because I don't think that's ever going away, but you are so afraid of what could happen that you weren't living in the moment of what was happening. And I couldn't breathe."

Everything she was saying was true. I hadn't even realized I was doing it. I was doing it right now. I had taken her to my house even though I had been planning to take her to the apartment to show her everything. But I wanted her in a place of security. A place I could control. Because people were after her, people were after me. The safest place she could be was not at my side, something we had done to ourselves in the first place. And yet I needed her to be safe. I needed to keep my eyes on her.

I was the fucking problem. I loved her so much, and watching her walk away, letting her walk away the first time had broken me. I wasn't sure I was going to be able to do it again.

"I...I'm sorry."

She shook her head then moved forward, putting her hands on my chest. The warmth seeped through my suddenly chilled skin and I swallowed, running my hands through her hair. I didn't even realize I was doing it until I looked down and saw those wide eyes. "I hate that you're sorry. Because you shouldn't be. It wasn't your fault. That's just how you're wired. And I know everything happening to your family hurt, and I tried to help. I tried to be by your side, but you didn't want to talk about it. You just wanted to put more security up and find out exactly who was hurting your family. You weren't talking to me about it. Along the way I needed to find out who I was before I could have someone as amazing as you. I'm just now realizing that I lost out on the best thing of my life and the best chance I had at happiness because I couldn't say that I need to figure it out without hurting you first. And that I'm sorry for."

I cursed, her words shocking some sense into me. Like the strike of a match, burning me from the inside out.

So I leaned down, taking her mouth. She tasted of dinner and wine and sweetness and everything that I had fucking missed. I had missed her mouth, her taste, her needs. I pulled away and swallowed hard, my breath coming in pants, her lips swollen. "That was probably the wrong fucking answer."

She shook her head, her hand digging into my shirt. "No, that's the right one. I think. Or maybe it is the wrong one. I don't know anymore."

I leaned down and kissed her again, needing her taste. Just needing her.

There was so much to talk about, so much we needed to go over, but it didn't matter. Not right then. I let her slide her hands up my shirt, her palms on my skin as I tugged on her hair, deepening the kiss. She moaned against me, both of us reaching for the other. We needed to talk, needed to go over it all but I didn't care. I missed this. I missed this so fucking much. I was like a dying man in a desert, craving temptation and salvation. And she was it. She was my everything. And now she was in my arms again.

I hadn't realized that I had pushed her towards the counter until her back reached it and we both froze. But without a word, I took her by the hips and lifted her onto the counter. She immediately wrapped her legs around my waist and I moaned, stripping off her shirt.

Her breasts were full, the lace cups barely containing them. I had always loved her tits, loved sucking on them, playing with them. She had let me fuck them over and over again, and she would lean down to lick the tip of my dick. It had been so hot, so fulfilling, and I missed those beautiful breasts.

"I'm glad you did," she whispered, and I realized I had said that last part out loud.

I didn't care, just leaned down and pressed a small kiss to the top of each globe before undoing the snap at the front.

Her bra slid to the floor, her breasts falling heavy into my palms. I pinched her nipples between my thumb and forefinger, rolling them as she leaned her head back and moaned, pressing her breasts more firmly into my hands. She gripped the edge of the counter and I continued to play with her breasts, licking and sucking at her nipples.

When she leaned forward, gripping my shirt, I jerked it over my head in one quick motion, loving the way that she panted as she looked at me. But then her gaze went to the bandage on my arm and I pinched her chin, forcing her to look at me.

"I'm fine."

"You just lifted me up on the counter. Did you hurt yourself?"

"I'm fine. Let me kiss you."

Let me love you.

But I didn't say that part out loud. Instead, I pulled at her leggings, loving the way that she immediately lifted her ass up, letting me pull them off her legs and toss them to the ground.

She had on peach lace panties and I groaned, leaning between her legs.

"So warm, so fucking sweet."

I pressed my nose against her clit through the lace, loving the way that she moaned again.

When I slid her panties to the side, I found her wet and swollen. So I sucked and I licked, moaning again as she rolled her hips along the counter, pressing her pussy against my face.

I spread her with two fingers, then used my other hand to play with her clit, my gaze on her cunt, then up at her face watching her eyes darken.

I dipped a finger deep into her cunt, loving the way that it squeezed my finger, before I pulled it out and reached up to her mouth. "Suck. Lick it clean."

She did as I asked, and for a moment I wondered if this was the controlling part, but I pushed those thoughts away.

We would deal with all of that. We would.

But right now, we needed this. Even if this was a big fucking mistake.

She sucked my finger clean, then I went back for more, spearing her with two fingers, my thumb on her clit. And when she came, I stood and captured her mouth, swallowing her shout for more.

It was my name on her lips that nearly sent me over the edge in my own jeans, but I held back, knowing we both needed this.

I undid my jeans and pushed my pants down below my ass, my cock springing free. She leaned forward and gripped me, stroking me once, twice.

"I missed this. I missed you."

The most beautiful words I'd ever fucking heard.

I positioned myself at the entrance of her sex and gripped the back of her neck, my thumb along her jawline. "Pull me in. Take me. All of me."

In more ways than one.

She arched her back, pressing the tip of my cock deep

inside her. I moved the rest of the way, thrusting slowly in and out, tantalizing, teasing.

And when I was seated to the base, both of us groaned.

"I've missed you," she whispered, her lips at my neck as she ran her hand over my hair. I did the same, just holding each other, stock still as her pussy pulsed around my cock.

And then we were moving, both of us breathing into one another, taking everything that we could.

Because this was probably a mistake. A memory and time of fractured silence. But it didn't matter. This was what I had missed. Her, everything. We fit in so many ways, but I had missed the parts where we hadn't. The fractured connections that had never made sense.

But I would fix that. I would find a way.

Because I loved her.

Even if I had fucked up beyond all recognition.

And when she came again, clamping around my dick, I followed her, filling her up, taking everything.

I'd find a way to fix this. Find a way to protect her. But that was for later.

Right now was one more mistake.

Right now was my second chance.

And probably my last.

Chapter Seven

Phoebe

The smart thing would've been to discuss what had happened. To talk out our feelings and decide what it all meant.

I had just had sex with my ex-boyfriend. The same ex-boyfriend that had been through so much with me, even in the past few days, that it felt like I was constantly catching up.

But did we talk about it? Of course not.

Instead I sat there at the edge of the counter, my legs wrapped around his waist, him still buried deep inside of me, and let out gasp after gasp, trying to catch my breath.

Because that was one of the things with Kane. He always took care of you. Even when you needed space to try to take care of yourself. He was always there to make sure you didn't fall. And to make sure you rose to the occasion.

I had orgasms before in my life, countless ones with my vibrator and my hand. But I had never had a real orgasm during sex like I had with Kane. I had thought those little slightly toe-curling, warming sensation bursts through my body during sex had been orgasms. No, that had just been a sneeze. A quick sensation that hadn't really gotten me there.

The blackout orgasms where it felt like I couldn't catch my breath, my whole body shook, my pussy clenched, and it felt as if my breasts were aching, the ones where light burst behind my eyelids, and I literally saw stars and maybe even God.

Those were the orgasms I got from Kane.

And I just had more than one sitting on his kitchen counter when we hadn't even discussed what the hell we were doing with each other.

Apparently pretending that we didn't care for each other and had no feelings for each other amounted to blow-your-head-off sex.

I sat with my arms still around him, afraid to say anything.

Because denial wasn't just a river in Egypt, and wasn't just what I felt day in and day out when it came to my feelings for Kane Montgomery Carr.

I was falling in love with him again, though could it be again when I never stopped?

This attraction was breaking us, or maybe just me.

Or maybe I needed to be honest with myself for the first time in far too long.

Then Kane slid his hands through my hair and looked into my face, cupping my cheek.

"Phoebe..."

His voice trailed off, and it made me feel a little bit better that both of us were out of our depths here.

We were making wrong decisions left and right, but at least we were doing it together?

I swallowed hard again. "I should—I think I need to clean up."

He nodded, then leaned forward. I was afraid he was going to kiss me, because if he kissed me, I would lean into him and pretend that nothing else hurt. That I hadn't bared my soul to him. That I hadn't been such an idiot in the past.

But he kissed my forehead.

He hadn't done anything wrong. And maybe I hadn't either. It had been the wrong time, the wrong place before, and perhaps it was again. I didn't have answers.

And I wasn't going to find them sitting on the counter with him still buried deep inside me.

When he pulled away, I felt the loss immediately. I

made my way to the back of the house to clean up, while he did the same in the kitchen.

I wanted to sleep in his arms, and I knew I needed a break. Needed to breathe.

But I stood in his bedroom, his robe wrapped around me, wondering what I was supposed to do.

He walked in and frowned at me.

"I think I have a pair of your pajamas here if you want them." He ran his hand through his hair. "I know I probably should have given them back to you. But, well, I probably should have done a lot of things."

"Kane," I whispered.

"No. Let's get some sleep. And text Claire where you're staying. That way she knows."

I nodded tightly. "You're right."

Kane let out a breath and moved forward to cup my face. I loved when he did that. It made me feel so safe, even though that was the exact opposite of why I had left to begin with. He was always there because I hadn't been able to find myself.

But I had. I had a job that I loved, and I had a network of friends outside of being in love with Kane. And he had been able to take care of himself.

But now it was all up in the air, and I didn't want to screw this up.

"Let's get some sleep, Phoebe. I can sleep on the

couch if you want. But I would prefer to sleep next to you. We'll figure it out in the morning. All of this. And I want to say that you're safe, but I don't want to overstep."

I shook my head. "No."

He took a step away before I reached out and grabbed his wrist. "I mean, the safety thing? It's a legitimate concern now. I'm not talking about before. So sleep next to me. And I guess we'll figure it out."

"I guess we will."

And then somehow I was in his arms, my robe on the floor, and we slept skin to skin, and when I felt his heartbeat underneath my cheek, I finally slept.

In my dreams there were no letters or phone calls, there was nothing chasing Kane. There were no screams and asphalt underneath us.

There was just him, his heartbeat, and everything I had missed. Everything I had given up because I was too scared. Too unsure of who I was.

And in my dreams, nothing mattered but him, me, and us.

I didn't want to wake up.

———

The next day I wasn't with Kane. That was probably a good thing because we both needed to get our heads on straight. It was hard to think when we were in the same room, when our pasts and presents collided in such an intricately entangled way.

I was at work, dealing with a few last-minute issues before I went out with a client. And because there was a legitimate concern for my safety, and because Kane was overprotective, though not in the way he had been in the past, Kingston was with me today.

I liked Kane's cousin. They looked somewhat alike in the way all the Montgomerys did. Most of them had dark hair naturally, though some of them dyed it whatever color they felt like. I dyed my hair a honey blond as it was, so I understood. Kingston also had blue eyes, but they were a slightly different shade than Kane's, and while they reminded me of the man that I still loved, they weren't exactly the same.

I enjoyed being around Kingston almost from the moment we met—the same day I met Kane. After all, Kingston and Claire were the reason that it had been easy for Kane and me to actually go out that first time.

As soon as I hung up with my client, I pinched the bridge of my nose. Kingston grunted.

He'd been sitting in the corner working on the count-less things he had to do with his job, and I wondered if he hated being forced to be a full-time bodyguard. I would hate it, because it meant that he couldn't actually do the work that he needed to do, because he was too busy babysitting me.

"Everything okay?" I asked, feeling as awkward as ever. Had Kane told him we slept together? Kingston had picked me up from Kane's house, so he probably figured it out. The man was observant after all. But maybe he thought Kane and I had slept in separate spaces. That I hadn't slept naked next to the man that I thought I would spend the rest of my life with. The fact that we were in a situation, not a relationship, was concerning. I had no idea what it meant. But none of that mattered in the light of day when we had other things to worry about.

"I'm trying to track the notes, but the police don't have his fingerprints, meaning the guy has never been run before, and he's not in the system. And the emails are being re-routed through three different IP addresses, and it's giving Noah fits. I said I would help take another look while I was sitting here with you."

I swallowed hard, my mouth going suddenly dry at the thought that whoever was doing this was far more sophisticated at it than I had thought.

"How do you run emails through IP addresses? I don't even know how to find mine."

He shook his head. "It's a process that some people can do quite easily. It's unraveling it that's the hard part, but Noah's usually decent at it. So I'm not sure what's going on."

From what little Kane had told me of the company, Noah was one of the best. The fact that he hadn't been able to trace the calls—nor had the detective in charge of my case—worried me. "I don't like this. I don't like the fact that you have to be here, or that someone is sending these weird notes. I mean, maybe they're just not dangerous? Maybe they're just playing a stupid game."

Kingston set down his tablet and moved towards me, a frown on his face. I straightened my shoulders back, not sure what he was going to do.

"The fact that they're doing all this rerouting worries me. That you went to Kane because you were scared? Trust that instinct. Maybe it's nothing, but you can't be too careful."

"And do you always have a one-on-one bodyguard for something like this? You're about to go on a client meeting with me. Doesn't that seem like we're overreacting?" I sighed. "I really want this just to be overreacting."

"Maybe it's overreacting and this is something that you can laugh about later. But I would rather us do too much than not enough." He swallowed, his gaze going distant for a moment as if he were remembering something he would rather not.

I knew some of what Kane had done. But because of

privacy reasons, and the way he always internalized things, I didn't know everything. He sometimes had bruises and cuts, but never went into any detail about how he got them. He always said it was the nature of his job, but I wanted to know more. And with Kingston right here? I wanted to make sure he was safe too.

Of course, that just made me a hypocrite because wasn't that why I had taken a step back from Kane? Because he needed to know that I was protected?

But who was protecting the Montgomerys?

"We do a lot in our job. A lot of times it's boring. It's setting up cameras or sitting outside a door during a meeting and waiting. I don't mind the boring parts. They mean we did our jobs right to begin with. And frankly, if Kane wanted me to sit on you for the entire day and make sure you didn't even get a paper cut? I'd do that. He's family. And he loves you."

I blushed, shaking my head. "Let's not talk about that, okay? It's far too complicated."

"Yes, because Kane totally slept on the couch last night." He rolled his eyes and held up his hands. "No, I'm not going to pry. I'd say it's none of my business, but it is because I'm a nosy asshole when it comes to my family. However, you both need to work your shit out. I told him that when you first broke up, but he was too fucking proud to do it. So maybe this is your second chance. I just really wish it wasn't while he was at the doctor getting his stitches checked out."

I dropped my phone. "What? He's at the doctor?" The panic in my voice made my words screech, and Kingston cursed.

"Shit. I wasn't supposed to tell you that."

"Why? Because I'm not supposed to worry about him? No, that's not how things work. His job is dangerous. I know that. But if I'm kept in the dark, then what does that make me? Just a fraction of his life that doesn't mean much? I don't need to know everything, but I need to know some things. Like the fact that he's not here because he's at the doctor. He was shot, Kingston. In my arms. I can still hear it echoing in my head. I can still hear my scream. He didn't scream. He didn't react other than to protect me. Because that's what he always does. So is he hurt? Did he have to go to the doctor for an emergency?" I asked, this time my voice far calmer and far more sure.

"It's just a checkup appointment. He should have told you, but he always wants to keep you in this little bubble and away from the decisions he makes at work."

"And we both know that precious little bubble popped. So maybe he should keep me updated."

"Are you two together? Do you have a right to know?"

I opened my mouth but was stopped by my phone ringing.

"That's a question I guess I'll have to answer later," I said before I went back to work. Kingston sighed. It looked like he wanted to say something else but refrained. That was good. I didn't have any answers.

I wasn't going to ask Kingston for them.

And I was truly afraid to ask Kane.

———

By the time I was finished with work, I was frazzled and tired. I hadn't slept much the night before, and it wasn't all to do with who I slept next to. Kingston followed me home, then made sure I was safe and locked up in my apartment with Claire before he gave us a two-finger salute and walked away.

I hadn't heard from Kane all day, other than a brief text message to check on me during lunch.

I wasn't even sure what I was supposed to say to him, because I needed to get my thoughts in order. Yelling at him because he hadn't told me he had gone to the doctor wasn't going to help anything. Kingston was right. Did I have the right to know?

I walked into the kitchen to find Claire there, a glass of wine in each hand.

I raised a brow at my best friend and roommate as she handed over a glass. "Tell me what happened."

"I think I made a mistake, or maybe not."

"That was very clear and concise. How about a few more details?"

I took a sip of my wine before explaining. "I slept with Kane." And then I took a big gulp. The sweet and tart taste covered my tongue, and I was grateful for the pinot grigio. At least it gave me something to do rather than blurt out everything else.

Claire blinked. "Okay. That's a start. Tell me every-thing." She gestured towards the couch and I sat down and told her everything that had happened, from start to finish. Including my conversation with Kingston. Claire set her half-finished wine glass on the coffee table and nodded. "He's right, you know. It's good that they're being overprotective. I like that we're more secure in this apart-ment. And while I think Kane should have told you he was going to the doctor since you were there for the inci-dent, it does bring up the question—what do you want?"

"I don't know. I don't know what I want. All I know is that I like him. I love him."

"If you love him, then talk to him about it."

"I did. I told him why I made that decision before. Why I think I made a mistake before."

Claire snapped her fingers and pointed at me. "There. Finally. You finally admit that you made a mistake by breaking up with Kane."

I set my wine glass down and put my hands over my face, screaming quietly for a moment. "Why didn't you tell me?" I let my hands fall, and Claire sighed.

"Because I thought you would snap out of it. It was what you needed at the time, but I thought the two of you would make it work if you would just talk to each other."

"It's so easy to talk to someone in a movie or in a book, but in real life? Do you know how hard it is to bare your soul to someone?"

Claire shook her head. "Not in that way. But you did. And then you slept with him. You love him. Do you trust him?"

"I trust him with everything that I am, except I don't trust him with himself. Does that make sense?" I asked.

Claire scrunched her nose. "Yes. So, talk to him about it."

"I will. Although he hasn't spoken with me today beyond that single text. So for all I know he thought it was a complete mistake. And we're never going to talk about it again. And it's over. Done."

"You will never know unless you ask. Which is the hardest thing, and super easy for me to say because I'm not in your shoes."

The doorbell rang, and I tensed, my knuckles turning white from how hard I clenched my hands.

"Let's check the camera. It's probably just a delivery,

you know my addiction to Amazon." She stood up and grabbed her phone, looking at the readout.

"It's a flower delivery guy. Do you want me to check?"

"No, I'll go to the door."

"How about I do it," Claire said as she moved past me, and alarms rocked through me. I shouldn't have to feel this fear. My so-called stalker just had to be someone playing a prank with too much time on their hands.

Only I wasn't sure that was the truth.

I heard Claire talking through the door, and then the door opened as she took the flowers from the man and signed something.

When she came forward, her eyes widened. "Well, Kane seems to be fine with it."

"What?"

"There's flowers here, they have to be from him, right?" she asked, before I looked at the note.

"They have to be from him." I wanted to feel warmth through my system, but neither one of us looked sure about that. Claire looked pale from where she stood in front of me holding the flowers.

Don't be afraid. I miss you. I'll see you soon. It took all within me not to drop the vase on the floor. I set it down, my hands shaking, and reached for my phone.

"I have to call Kane. This guy sent flowers. I really wanted these to be from Kane. I really wanted my only worries in life to be about my relationship, my family, and my deadbeat dad. I did not want this."

"I'll call Kane for you. It's okay. We've got this. I checked the guy's ID though, he's literally from the florist."

"What florist?" I asked, my head shooting up.

"I wrote everything down just like Kingston told me to. We'll handle this. Maybe the guy made a mistake. Maybe he paid with a credit card and left his name."

She dialed Kane from my phone and I rolled my shoulders back, taking the phone from her so I could handle it myself. I realized it wasn't going to be that easy.

Something was wrong. This guy was escalating. And I wasn't sure what I was supposed to do. But I knew who would.

I just swallowed hard before I said, "Kane? He sent flowers."

I trusted him. I always had. Just not necessarily with my heart, or his. But that didn't matter right now.

Not when danger lurked far too close.

Chapter Eight

Kane

"Thanks again for picking me up."

Crew grinned as he signaled to turn left. "I don't mind. I love that Daisy stole your car because Hugh stole hers."

I rolled my eyes, doing my best not to jostle my shoulder. It had been a few days since everything happened and I still had stitches but it wasn't too sore. I couldn't believe I had been shot—again. The first time had been worse, and was something I still hadn't told Phoebe about. We hadn't been together at the time, but when she'd asked about the scar, I distracted her with my mouth.

I had been good at distracting her because I hadn't wanted to scare her. And then my life had brought it all into focus, even when we hadn't been together. That, and the fact that some asshole had sent her letters and calls. No, hiding things from her hadn't helped. Clearly, since that was why she broke up with me.

I had been so in her life, but not involved enough. How was I supposed to change that? How was I supposed to keep her safe without being overprotective?

That just didn't compute.

"Hugh's car is in the shop for a recall of some sort, and what was supposed to be an hour-long thing is now taking three days."

Crew snorted. "So, Hugh took Daisy's car so they could get Lucy to school and shit. And then, what, Daisy just carjacked you?"

"Pretty much. It all worked out in the end I guess. Though I love how she called you to pick me up and not any of the other one hundred family members I have."

Crew sighed. "Because I owed her. Apparently she wanted to cash in her chips."

"You guys are the weirdest exes I've ever met," I said dryly.

"We weren't together very long, and we're better as friends. Of course, that is a lovely segue to the fact that I guess I can't ask out Phoebe, since you're together again?"

I turned to glare at him as we sat at the stoplight. "Excuse me?" An irrational urge to punch the man who was driving me back to the office slammed into me.

"I was just kidding. Hell. I wanted to see how you would react. So, you and Phoebe are really together again?"

"What are we? Little old ladies with tea and gossip?" I hedged.

"I like tea. Plus, you get those little sandwiches with cream cheese. I don't see the problem with that. And it's not gossip. I'm asking if you're with Phoebe again. You got all mopey when you broke up."

"I wasn't mopey."

"No? Wait, you didn't break up with her, did you? She dumped your ass."

"Crew, why does Daisy put up with you?"

"Because I'm handsome, I can fight, and I'm like glue. I stick real well."

"That's not even a saying." I rolled my eyes and leaned back into the seat. "And yes, Phoebe dumped me. Apparently I am overprotective and didn't share enough of myself. So she wasn't able to figure out who she was when I was always in her space. I didn't realize I was a fucking stalker." I hadn't realized I snapped out the words until Crew whistled through his teeth.

"Well, hell. You're in Montgomery Security, and you may not have the last name, but you're a fucking Montgomery. Of course you're going to be overprotective.

That's sort of how things work with your family. Daisy sure is."

"You should come work with us. You're as growly as we are."

"Yes, but I have no need to do that. I work with my hands in other ways," the guy teased and I sighed.

"I fucked up."

"I'm sure you did. But about what?"

I reached out and punched him in the shoulder, and he laughed. "You're lucky you're injured and feeble or I'd punch you back."

"There's nothing feeble about me."

"Don't get your pride all hurt. I just picked you up from getting your bullet wound checked. So, excuse me if I think that you're injured. Maybe not feeble, I'm sorry for using that word. But you did get shot. Is that what you're talking about fucking up with? Or are we going back to Phoebe?"

I pinched the bridge of my nose. "I think both? Hell."

"Okay, let's talk about Phoebe first because I like her."

"Watch your step."

"I didn't mean *like* like her. I have my eyes on someone else. Just so you know."

Intrigued, I leaned forward. "So, you really are over Daisy?"

"I don't know what is with you guys thinking that me

and Daisy were ever anything more than a few nights of fun. Plus, she's in love with that British dude and could be a stepmom any day now. Seriously, Hugh and Daisy are perfect for each other. I like the guy. And he doesn't want to punch me every time he sees me, so he clearly knows that Daisy and I aren't meant for each other. And yes, I have my eyes on someone else. Not that she sees me at all. But we're not talking about me. We're talking about you. So, Phoebe dumped your ass. That makes sense. You never share your feelings."

"There's a lot in that statement that I want to go over, but why the hell would I share my feelings with you?"

"Because we're friends. And you literally are sitting next to me wanting to talk about it."

"Maybe." I let out a breath. "I don't know how. I thought I was doing everything right. We dated, we went out, we slept over at each other's places, I told her how much I wanted her, and how much I liked her in my life. Isn't that enough?"

"Did you talk about your job?"

"Of course I did," I said softly.

"Okay, beyond the aspects of, 'Hey, I put up security things and sometimes I have a gun?'"

"Why did you say that in a sing-song voice?" I asked.

"Because your job scares the shit out of me. I may train with Daisy, but I could never do what you guys do."

"It's not always dangerous."

"Says the man with a bullet wound."

"That doesn't happen often."

"But it does enough that your team has a to-do list and a step-by-step plan if someone gets attacked. And you're dealing with a lot of things that are outside of just a security camera set up at someone's private home. Did you talk to Phoebe about any of that?"

"There are things I can't talk about."

Crew was silent for a minute before he sucked in another breath through his teeth. "Sure. But did you talk about *any* of it? Because if you say she's feeling overprotected, it's probably because you did that Montgomery guy thing where you want to protect the little woman and put her on a pedestal. Which, I get it. I'm the same way. But you also probably didn't share anything that you were feeling. I know, I know, this whole getting in touch with your feelings thing coming from me is pretty ironic. But maybe you should talk to her about it."

"About what, about the fact that if I had just caught the guy to begin with when we were in that building, if I hadn't let him get away because I was trying to protect Daisy, my family wouldn't be in the crosshairs of a Sherman Company dude? A guy with a gun who decided to just come after us because he thought he was better than us?"

I hadn't realized I was feeling like that until the words were already out.

Crew didn't say anything, and finally I whistled. "Well, hell."

"I don't know everything, I don't know the details, but if you were rescuing Daisy and anyone else, is that really a mistake you think you made?"

"Sherman's still out there."

"He's a little pissant who didn't like that your company was bringing in bigger clients and doing a better job. I remember Daisy saying that they were always trying to outmaneuver you guys. And then it turns out that they were the ones that helped blow up the building Daisy was in? That man's insane. That's not on you."

"But I taunted him," I blurted.

Crew frowned. "When?"

"Years ago. It was right when we were deciding to start our company. We were just getting out of training, and the guy came over to us, treating us like shit, saying something ignorant to Ford and Noah, even though they weren't even dating at the time. So I riled him up. I taunted him. I don't even remember what I said, but the guy has had it out for us ever since."

I hadn't realized the guilt had been there until the words were out, but it was there. Maybe if I hadn't been such an asshole, none of this would've happened. That was the story of my fucking life.

"It's not your fault. The guy said something ignorant, of course you're going to push back. You protect what's yours. I know you, Kane. You wouldn't have said anything completely crass or out of pocket. So, what did Tim Sherman do after that?"

"He got all red-faced and said that the Montgomerys would be nothing, and he would take our next client." I frowned. "And then he tried to poach from us, and succeeded a few times."

"And somehow that escalated him into making deals with the wrong people."

"Then he shot at us. He could have killed Phoebe."

"Do you think he's the same one that is stalking her?" he asked, and I shook my head.

"No, the police don't think so, and neither do we. Jennifer and Kate did linguistics and it doesn't even sound like him."

"Well, that's something."

"Is it? That means there's someone else after her."

"But the guy stalking her doesn't seem dangerous, right?"

I gritted my teeth. "Bothering her and scaring her is dangerous enough."

"You're right. I didn't mean to make light of it. So, no leads then?"

"None. And it's frustrating me all to hell. Whoever this guy is, he's good with computers. It's the only way he could be hiding his IP addresses like that. Phoebe has gone over everybody that she has spoken to in the past year that she can think of with the authorities and us, and no one is hitting any triggers. Nothing's sparking. I don't like that somebody is in her business like that, freaking her out."

"It'd be freaking me out," Crew said honestly. "So, are you guys just going to be one-on-one with her until you find this guy? Even with Tim on the loose?"

"For now. We have security at her place and her work, but she's not always in her office. And I can't put her in a little box and keep her safe and wrapped away and hidden from the world. That's not how life works. And that's sure as hell not how her job works."

"Did you tell her that?"

I frowned and looked over at Crew.

"What do you mean?"

"Did you tell her that you didn't want to put her in a little box? She might like hearing that. Especially with what you said had been worrying her."

I sighed and leaned against the seat as we made our way towards the office.

"Yeah. I should. Damn it. I'm not good at this thing."

"By 'this thing' you mean a relationship? I'm not good at them either. I don't know why you're taking any advice from me."

That made me laugh, and when we pulled into the parking lot of Montgomery Security, I looked over at him. "You're right. Why am I taking advice from you?"

"No clue. Come on, I'm going to go get coffee and I want to go talk to Leif about some ink."

I liked that his eyes lit up at that, and I followed him towards the building that my family owned.

My family wasn't a million-dollar conglomerate or anything like that, we just had a lot of people who happened to own a lot of small businesses. My cousins and I owned Montgomery Security, which happened to be in the same building as Montgomery Ink Legacy, which my other cousins owned. Of course, that was next to Latte on the Rocks, which wasn't owned by a Montgomery—technically. Although Greer was dating Ford and Noah, and Raven had married Sebastian, so I guess it was now Montgomery owned. And the art studio and showcase next door was owned by even more of my family. Somehow we had combined all of our likes and work-life into this place where we could actually see each other instead of only at family reunions, which we didn't have as often as we used to.

There were just too many of us, and it wasn't like we could rent a town hall every time we wanted to have a dinner together.

Maybe it hadn't been smart to put our home office next to our family. At first it had only been because we needed the space and it was available. And it wasn't like we brought dangerous people into our place of business. But things had happened, and not just with Montgomery Security, that made the building sometimes a target. I didn't know the solution for that, other than we were doing our best to keep each other safe.

"Hey, you okay?" Crew asked, and I nodded.

"Yeah, just wool-gathering."

"Well, gather wool later. Let's go get some coffee from your in-laws."

I didn't correct him on the family connection. My younger sister Allison was my only sister. While Daisy was my cousin, not a second or third cousin, the rest of them were technically separated by more than just one line on the family tree. But our generation didn't care about that too often. We were all cousins, siblings, and everyone that married in we either called a cousin or an in-law. It helped the family dynamic without having to put a specific label on everyone.

Raven, Sebastian's wife, was behind the counter at Latte on the Rocks, and grinned at us as we walked in.

Her dark hair was pulled back and I noticed she had put in a few more hot pink streaks.

I loved the way Raven lit up a room, and that she had been so good for Sebastian. He had been through hell and back, and had lost everything once, but now they were raising a beautiful daughter, and I knew they were only just beginning their lives together.

"Crew. Kane, how'd your appointment go?" Raven asked, and I frowned.

"Fine, but how did you know I had one?"

"Family group chat." Raven rolled her eyes. "I don't know why you're surprised that we all know everything. It's sort of what the family does."

I winced. "Hell. Do you think someone told Phoebe?"

Raven raised a pierced brow. "Probably, considering she's with Kingston right now."

I wasn't even going to ask how she knew that. I ignored Crew's knowing look and pulled out my phone. "I should probably tell her I'm okay."

"You didn't tell her that you had an appointment today?" Raven asked, disappointment clear on her features.

I ignored her, and knew I'd have to apologize later. As I went to dial, Phoebe's name and face popped up on my screen before I had a chance to do anything. It was an old photo, taken on the day we met. It was just a quick shot of the two of us, one that Claire had taken as a joke to memorialize the moment that a bear had tried to murder us. Those had been her words, and I had laughed and had leaned into Phoebe.

I hadn't realized at that moment that I had already started to fall in love with her. I answered quickly as Crew went to order a coffee.

"Hey, I was just calling you to tell you how my appointment went." Not quite a lie, and I counted that as progress, right? That I wasn't hiding things? Shit. This relationship thing was harder than I thought.

"Kane? Kingston just dropped me off at the apartment. I'm here alone with Claire, all locked up, but I just got flowers. I thought they were from you, but they aren't. They're from him. And I don't know what to do."

My jaw clenched, and from the way Crew and Raven both looked at me, I knew they saw the fury on my features.

"I'm heading over. I'll call Kingston, you call the detective. I'm on my way. Stay safe. Okay, babe?"

"It's okay. It's just flowers. He's not here." She continued to talk and I swallowed hard, holding my rage in again. I knew if I didn't, I'd crack the phone in my hands.

"I'm coming, Phoebe. I promise."

"I know. I know, Kane. I'll be here."

I hung up and looked over at Crew. "I'm going to need a ride."

Crew nodded, and I knew that I would destroy the world to protect Phoebe. The woman that I loved.

I couldn't believe I had been standing in my own way this whole time. But in the end it didn't matter. Someone was out to get her. Someone had scared her.

And I would end them.

Somehow.

Chapter Nine

Phoebe

After the police left, I sat on my couch, Claire next to me, as I watched Kane pace my living room. As soon as I had called him, I knew it had been the right thing to do. Because whoever was bothering me, sending me those calls and messages, had escalated. That's exactly what it was. But now it seemed like I was worrying him. I was scared. I could admit that, but I hated the fact that Kane, even in pain, looked worried right along with me.

"Did you guys eat?" he asked, and I blinked, realizing that we hadn't, and I hadn't even asked him if he needed anything to drink.

I quickly stood up, running my hands over my hips as if to wipe off the clamminess.

"No, let me make us something."

"I can do it," Claire said, as she reached out and squeezed my hand. "You two talk. We're okay. Promise."

Kane looked between us and nodded. "I know you are. You guys are good. I'm just trying to not freak the fuck out and stress you guys out so just let me be a little alpha male and growly right now."

"I can do that," Claire said with a laugh, and then she gave him a quick hug. Kane's arms moved to reach around her automatically, hugging her back. That made me smile. Because even with everything that was happening, Claire was still friends with Kane. She had hung out with the Montgomerys, especially Kingston, since he and their other cousin Aria were with Kane more often than not.

They were a team. And I knew that Claire missed hanging out with them.

Just like I missed them.

"You don't have to go to any trouble," Kane said softly as Claire took a step back, a flush on her cheeks.

"No, I was just going to heat up leftovers. I'm not going all out."

That made me laugh. "It's either that or take out." I shuddered. "Though I'm not sure I'm ready for delivery."

Kane scowled, and then moved forward to take my hand. I let out a soft sigh, having missed his touch. I knew I should probably take a step back and figure out if falling into each other like this during a crisis on both sides was a mistake, but I didn't want to. Because even in the short months we had been apart, I had changed, and I thought maybe he had as well. Perhaps I needed to stop overthinking it because there was already enough to overthink.

"I'll go reheat them," Claire said as she scurried to the kitchen and I shook my head.

"I think she's trying to give us privacy, but our apartment is not that big."

"I'm actually just hungry," Claire called out, confirming my statement.

I laughed and moved to wrap my arms around Kane.

"So, any updates beyond what the authorities said?"

He shook his head. "There's nothing that they can do. The guy paid with cash, so they're keeping an eye on things." He scowled. "Fucking pisses me off."

"Same," I said.

"I was going to tell you about the doctor's appointment, by the way. They were just checking the stitches. I'm fine. The fact that I didn't wear the sling like I should have meant that they yelled at me, but I'm good. Crew dropped me off."

"I'm sorry that he didn't come in so we could feed him leftover pasta." I tried to smile, to make it a joke, but I saw the worry in his gaze. I hated that, even though it was justified.

"Anyway," I said after a moment. "Thank you for

telling me. I'm trying to get back into the habit of telling you everything, too."

"I only had a half-day at work today, even though I've been doing a bunch of online shit, researching. I'm taking a class."

My eyes widened. "A class?"

"Just keeping updated on the cyber aspect of our jobs. Things are changing constantly, and I want to keep up. It's my turn, since Kingston took it last time." His lips twitched. "Kingston hates those classes."

"I could see that," I replied, thinking of his cousin. While Kane was growly, Kingston usually put on a smile and joked around. But I always thought he was a little more guarded than he let on. Far more growly.

"Okay, I heated up our food, and now I'm going to go sit in my room and watch TV and pretend that a man who is being really creepy to Phoebe didn't send flowers today. And the fact that I didn't just open the door and nearly let a random stranger in even though I had the guard on the door."

I heard the worry in her tone and moved forward. "You don't have to go in your bedroom."

"I want to give you guys some space, and I really just want to get comfy under the covers."

"You didn't do anything wrong," Kane added, and I was grateful. Because I knew Claire felt guilty even though she hadn't done anything, and nothing had happened.

"I should have just had him leave it at the door."

"But it was an actual delivery man who signed in through the doorman below. You didn't do anything wrong, and we're going to be extra careful in the future. Don't put this on yourself. It's on that man. And we're going to find him."

Claire sighed and smiled, though it didn't quite reach her eyes. "I know you will. Don't worry. You've got this. I trust you."

Then she scampered off to the bedroom, closing the door behind her. I tugged Kane to the kitchen island.

"Can we just sit on a stool here and talk? I'm starving."

He looked down at the leftover pasta and artichokes on his plate and frowned. "No meat?"

I rolled my eyes. "Sorry, protein's expensive."

"I'll cook you a steak next time. You need the iron."

"Okay. But there's iron in things other than steak." I paused. "I could really use a steak. Not that this pasta wasn't great fresh, though it's probably not going to be amazing reheated."

He shrugged, then leaned over the counter to kiss me. "I don't care. I'm starving and I just want to be next to you. I'm not leaving, okay? I'll sleep on the couch."

I met his gaze. "No. Stay. With me."

He smiled softly, then sat at the other side of the counter and dug in. It didn't look like he hated the leftover pasta, and while it wasn't exactly perfect food, it was just what I needed. Comfort, and no extra work.

"Sorry for being a bitch about the no meat thing," he grumbled.

"You're a carnivore, it's fine. I should have remembered."

He shrugged, then winced at the movement. I wanted to reach out but considered if he would be receptive to that.

"The doctor said that I'm fine to do normal activities, I'll just be a little sore. The bullet didn't dig in too far, but it bled a lot; that's why it freaked us both out."

"So you're going to be okay?"

He met my gaze, the seriousness in his heartening. "Yes. And I have been. We still can't find Tim though."

I blinked, shocked that he was sharing with me. Something he hadn't actually done much in the past. It had taken me looking back at our relationship to realize that he had always held himself apart, like what he did was too scary for me. But he was talking about it more now. He went into detail about Sherman Security, and I listened intently. They were still searching for the man who had tried to hurt the Montgomerys. There had been more to it, another client who wanted to take out Daisy, and I was grateful that Daisy and everyone else was safe. But there was still one man evading the police and authorities because of his training.

"I'm pretty sure he used to be a mercenary. Which freaks me the fuck out because I have no idea if he's even going to be staying in the States. Because as soon as he crosses a border, as soon as he's done with us? They're not going to catch him."

"Then maybe it's good he's gone. I know it sucks there won't be any resolution, but I don't want him to hurt you guys."

"But that also means that we failed." He scraped the last bit of cheese off the plate and chewed.

"You didn't fail if you don't catch him. It's not your job."

"Yeah, well, tell that to me after I've stayed up too late trying to go over every single interaction we ever had to see if I fucked up."

I was still shocked that he was sharing so much; this was so different. Maybe this *was* different. Maybe we were. And maybe I was thinking too hard about it.

"What does Kingston have to say about all of it?" I asked as I started to clean up. He stood and took the plates from my side, rinsing them in the sink. I rolled my eyes, then went to wipe off the counter. I loved that he didn't expect me to do dishes or anything like that, like a former boyfriend of mine had. He had literally said the phrase "barefoot and pregnant in the kitchen" at one point, which had been the last straw. Kane was never like that. He was raised by good people who made sure that he treated women right. I just wish he would have been able to share more of himself in the past.

"Kingston is taking it on more than I am, which says something." He rolled his eyes. "He is back at the office with Ford going through paperwork, seeing if we can figure out where Tim might be holed up. And he's working on your case."

"I still can't believe I have a case. I mean, every once in a while I would get a note, then he would go quiet for a while, but now flowers? It's just unnerving. And I want to say he doesn't seem dangerous, but I don't like that he's doing it at all. And the idea that he's smart enough that we can't catch him right away? It creeps me out."

With soapy hands, Kane reached out and pushed my hair from my face.

"I'm not leaving. I'm going to be here, okay?"

"I know. I know." I went to my tiptoes and kissed him. He smiled against my lips before he kissed me back. Then my phone buzzed, and he sighed. "Probably a good thing. Because I think fucking you on your kitchen island with your roommate in the next room probably isn't a good idea."

I rolled my eyes, my cheeks heating because just the idea of him fucking me on the kitchen counter again made me want to press my thighs together.

But there was a time and a place.

Isabella: *I'm just thinking of you. Did you eat? Any updates? Let's do family dinner. I love you.*

"Who is it?" Kane asked, and he didn't sound worried, just interested. Like a boyfriend would be.

Not like the overprotective grouchy man that he had sometimes been.

"Isabella." I looked over at him as he rolled his eyes. "What?" I asked with a laugh.

"She hates me."

"She doesn't hate you."

"I hurt her little sister. She'd have me on a rotisserie, spinning over a fire pit if she could."

That visual made me shiver. "Oh no. She would bury you alive. That's a lot more fulfilling for her than having to do the extra labor of burning you alive and having to deal with the smell." I said it so deadpan that Kane blinked at me before he winced.

"Okay, well that's something I never needed to know."

"Sorry."

"You're not sorry at all, but I don't mind."

"Let me just text her back."

"Are you going to tell her I'm here?" he asked, his voice soft. "Or about the flowers?"

I cringed. "I'll tell her you're here, but I'm a little worried about the flower part."

"Well, that does make me feel better," he said, and I heard the honesty in that.

Me: *Everything's good. I just finished dinner. Kane's here.*

My phone immediately rang and I rolled my eyes.

"Big sisters," I said with a laugh, but I answered as Kane gestured for me to do so.

"Hello there, Isabella."

"Kane's there? Why is he there? Is everything okay? Was there another attack?"

It hadn't even occurred to me that's where her mind had gone, though it should have. I was an idiot. Or I was love drunk over the fact that Kane was in my kitchen.

"He's here because we had dinner, and then I was going to go make out with him on the couch later while watching a movie. Hope that's okay with you."

I was completely distracting her from the fact that I had a stalker. Not that she knew that part. If possible, she would kidnap me and keep me safe in her house where nobody could ever hurt me. She would do that to all of us, including our mother, if she had a chance. I'm not sure if she would do the same to Dad. Isabella and the rest of my siblings knew our dad more than I did, since he had stayed with them longer. I only had a small relationship with him. I mean I loved him, he was my dad, but Isabella and my mom were the ones that raised me.

"So, you're together again." She paused, and I waited to hear the lecture. Only it didn't come, which surprised me. "Okay. Tell him hi for me, and if he hurts you, I will gut him. Or something worse. Actually, I'll have to figure out something because he's highly trained so I'm going to do something that surprises him. Don't tell him that I'm thinking about how to do that."

"Isabella, you're a nut."

"Maybe, but I'm a protective nut. Now I have to go back to work because a deadline waits for no one, but I love you. Stay safe, and just well...Phoebe?"

"Yes?"

"Be happy, okay? Kane used to make you happy. I hope he continues to do so."

I swallowed the lump in my throat, grateful she couldn't see me. But Kane could, and when he frowned at me, reaching forward to wipe the tear from my cheek, I leaned into his palm, needing his warmth.

"I love you, you know."

"I love you too, baby sister. Now, be safe and use a condom."

Kane burst out laughing and I realized it was because he was so close he could hear that.

Isabella laughed on the other side, and repeated the phrase, and I said I loved her again before hanging up.

"She's ridiculous."

Kane raised a brow. "Well, sadly I don't have a condom on me."

My cheeks burned again. "Well, I have some in my bedroom. We should go in there and check. Just to make sure they're still there."

"That was smooth, babe."

"I try. Seriously though? I'm really surprised that Isabella was so cool with that."

"You're an adult. And I like the fact that she is protective of you. Even though I'm trying not to be too much."

"As long as I can be equally as protective of you, and as long as we talk about it, I'm okay. I promise."

And that was the truth, even though I was once again worried I was making a mistake. Because things weren't perfect, but they felt good in this moment. Maybe that's exactly what I needed. When his lips captured mine, I set my phone down and leaned into him.

"I'm glad you're staying."

"I wouldn't want to be anywhere else," he whispered. "We can deal with everything else later."

I trusted him. Because we would deal with it. He had already begun to.

Things wouldn't be like before. I just had to ignore the fact that two people were coming at us, scaring us, but we would fight that. We'd find a way through it.

I wasn't sure what I would do if we didn't.

Chapter Ten

Kane

"Put your hands over your head and arch your back. Spread those legs for me."

I licked my lips as I bent between Phoebe's open thighs, spreading her delicate folds. She was all warm and wet and mine. I didn't have much time, I had to be quick, but I needed to savor her.

I loved eating a woman out. Scratch that, I loved eating Phoebe out. She was a feast, a glorious indulgence of sweetness and tartness blended on my tongue.

"Kane." Her breaths were a moan, her body soft and pliant beneath me.

"I've got you. Just let go."

I spread her folds, looking down at her pussy. She was so pink, flushed, and I knew with just a lick and a slight touch I could send her over the edge. I loved watching

Phoebe come. It made me groan, it made me want more. But it was all I could do not to just go too fast like we always did. I needed this moment to last, even though we didn't have that kind of time.

I gently slid my thumb over her folds, spreading her before going back to her clit, and she shuddered in my hold. I continued to tease her, slowly using my forefinger to slide inside her wet cunt. She was hot, tight, and when she clamped down around me, I used her wetness to roll my thumb over her clit again.

She arched against me as I knelt on the floor at the edge of the bed between her spread thighs.

She was a beautiful sight that morning, something I would remember to the end of my days.

This was how I wanted to wake up. With Phoebe on my mouth, ready to come, and ready to start our day.

"I'm famished. This is the best fucking breakfast."

She giggled softly, and then there were no more words. My mouth was on her and we were both groaning. She licked her lips as she leaned up to watch what I was doing, but I pressed her back down on the bed, my hand on her breast, the other teasing her with my fingers. I had my mouth on her, and then she was coming, her cunt clamping around my fingers.

She whispered my name, the sensation nearly too much.

I pulled out of her, slid my hands over her thighs, and flipped her on her stomach.

"Kane!" she gasped and I grinned. She looked over her shoulders, flipping her hair, and I did the only thing I could do.

I slammed into her from behind.

Her eyes widened, her mouth parting into a little O, and I stood there, balls deep in my woman, and groaned out a breath.

"So fucking amazing," I gritted out before I pulled out of her, her wetness coating my dick, before slamming back into her again. She threw her head back, meeting me thrust for thrust.

That morning I couldn't feel the ache in my shoulder, couldn't remember my own fucking name except for when she called it out. All that mattered was that my woman was surrounding my cock and I was pounding into her.

I was claiming her in the best ways possible.

And when my thumb slid across her ass, over that little puckered hole, she shivered in my hold.

"Next time," I grumbled, and she looked over her shoulder again, sweat sliding down her back.

"Only if I can do that to you," she teased.

I groaned. "Let's talk about that later," I hedged, but she just laughed.

The fact that we could laugh while doing this, that had to mean something.

Or I was losing my damn mind.

It didn't matter, all that did was her. With one hand playing with her breasts, her nipples hard points against my palm, I slid my other hand around to play with her clit. She arched up, and I pulled her back to my front, so she was on her knees at the edge of the bed, and I was sliding in and out of her as I stood behind her.

"Come for me. Come on my cock." Her skin heated beneath my hands and my back tingled, my balls tightening at the edge of bliss, needing to come with her.

"Kane." She turned her head so we were kissing, my hands sliding over her, her hands reached over her shoulder to run her fingers through my hair.

"I've got you," I whispered, and then she was coming, squeezing my cock, and I followed her, filling her, the motion tightening my balls, that sensation at the base of my spine meaning that I was done, spent, all hers.

We collapsed in a tangle of limbs. My dick still deep in her, as she caught her breath.

I opened my mouth to say something, anything, though I didn't know what it would be, when my alarm went off.

We both froze, before I chuckled roughly, her shoulders shaking.

"Well, it's not like we really needed to sleep."

I kissed her shoulder, sliding my hands down her side.

"Sleep is overrated."

In the weeks since the flowers had arrived at her house, nothing else had happened.

Nothing but us falling into a routine where it felt like we were making this work, or at least trying.

There had been no more calls, no more notes, no more flowers.

There was nothing except the dread of wondering what would happen next, and when.

We wanted to believe that the guy had given up because we had increased security so much, but life wasn't always like that.

The fact that we were still hunting for Tim was evidence of that.

There hadn't been a peep from the man, and perhaps he had left the country. Maybe he realized shooting at us had been one step too far for him, but I didn't believe that.

Both of these people were waiting, and I didn't like that.

Especially because I was ninety-nine percent sure that these weren't even connected.

That meant there were two people out there trying to hurt my family.

And Phoebe was my family.

Even if neither one of us was ready to admit it.

"We should shower." She paused. "Separately. And then I have work."

I kissed her shoulder and slid out of her.

"I have a meeting and a security setup." I paused. "And then dinner tonight still? Unless you have that meeting?" I asked, feeling awkward.

Because in those weeks, the routine we had fallen into had become a full-on relationship. I was trying to be more open, but Phoebe? She had always been open. She always told me what she felt.

I just needed to listen better.

And not be the grumpy asshole that I was really good at being.

Tonight though, tonight was something that we had avoided since entering back into each other's lives with a literal bang. Because tonight was dinner with my family.

I loved my family. They were amazing, caring, and were some of the best people I knew. They put family first, were brilliant, and were just good people.

And they loved Phoebe.

And though I knew my family loved me, they had always wondered aloud what I had done to screw up the relationship.

The fact that they had been right annoyed me.

"Yes. I miss your parents. And your sister."

Phoebe slid the sheet above her, covering herself and, while I missed the view, I knew that we needed to get going for the day.

"I just don't want you to be nervous."

She bit her lip and shook her head. "No, I'm not. Okay, I am, only because I don't want them to hate me. I feel like a horrible person."

I frowned. "Why would you feel like a horrible person? My family loves you."

"They did. They welcomed me with open arms when we first started dating. I love your parents. Your mom is brilliant, and the best baker that I know."

My lips twitched. "I did have the best birthday cakes when I was a kid."

"And your dad? Talk about a hot zaddy."

I shuddered, as we walked into the bathroom to get ready for the day.

"Please don't say that when I'm naked. No, let's change that up. Never say that about my father."

"I'm just saying, Dimitri Carr is one hot man."

"I'm going to ask you once again to never say that," I said deadpan.

"I just feel like I let them down. They welcomed me into their home, and then we broke up. Or I broke up with you."

I stepped into the shower and frowned, looking over at her.

"We don't have to keep bringing that up you know," I said gently. "The who-broke-up-with-who thing. We're both trying. We're talking it out. You do not have to feel guilt over that."

And that was the truth. Because she had been right, I had been holding back. And, honestly, I hadn't realized I loved her until she was gone. And that was a fucking problem. One that I was working on. Something I should have been doing to begin with. And the fact that I hadn't meant that the break had been good for us.

Even though it had torn something from me.

"It's really hard to disagree with you when you're all wet and naked in there," she said, and I laughed.

"I'm going to have to do that more often. Seriously though, my parents love you. Allison loves you. And she misses you," I said, speaking of my younger sister.

"I miss her too. I just, I just don't want them to hate me."

I tugged her into the shower with me, towel and all, and kissed her hard on the mouth. Water slipped over both of us and I sighed. "They can't hate you. I never did." Though I had told myself I hated her. It had been easier than admitting to myself I loved her.

"I don't want them to feel bad though. Or feel weird."

"They're going to feel weird because they are weird. They're my parents." I paused. "And can we please be dressed the next time we talk about them. This is weird."

"Okay, fine. Now, seriously, you're all wet and naked and it's very hard for me to think."

I looked between us, at my very hard cock, and her very pert nipples, and licked my lips.

"We might have to be late for work."

"Kane Montgomery Carr!" she called out, and then she wasn't speaking anymore because I was on my knees, one of her legs over my shoulder and her cunt pressed to my mouth.

I couldn't help it. I had slipped.

And we were indeed late for work.

———

"So, they think he is in Brazil of all places," Kingston said from where he sat at his desk, across from my desk, in the office. He sipped his coffee while I glared at mine. Everyone else was out of office except for Kate, our admin. She was up front handling the thousand things she did during a day. I wasn't sure how she did it, but she made sure I didn't have to do any of it. Because before we had Kate, and after Aria left, it had been up to me and Noah, and that hadn't always worked out well. Noah was decent but I was only organized when it came to my shit. Not others' shit.

Right now, though, with Kate working up front and the rest of the team out on assignment, I was alone to glare at my cousin. "Brazil? They think he's in Brazil?"

"That's what my contact says. They're handling it because it's an FBI issue. Sometimes I really wish we were like fucking 007 or mercenary security dudes who could go into a burning building, knock down the door, and save the day."

"We aren't Jason Statham." I paused. "Wait, which Jason Statham movie would that be if we were mercenaries and knocking down doors?"

We each looked at each other and said, at the same time, "All of them."

My lips twitched before I sipped my coffee. "I wish we could handle it ourselves. I don't like that he's going to get away."

"He's out of our hair though. He doesn't have access to the technology or the guy who knew how to work the technology. Because his cyber guy is behind bars."

"That's a small mercy."

"He's behind bars, and so are the others. We're just looking for this last one, and the FBI's on it."

"Then why did he come out and shoot me? He could have killed Phoebe."

"Because he was desperate."

"I should have gotten him then. I'm trained, I'm faster than that."

"And you would've left Phoebe alone in the parking lot while you were bleeding. I shouldn't have let you leave alone when we knew he was still out there."

"I just don't like any of it, nor do I like the fact that Daisy is working with Phoebe today because Phoebe had a meeting outside of the office."

Because it had been a few weeks, we had decided, mostly thanks to Phoebe talking me down, that when she was in the office or at home, and as long as her security system was up, she didn't need one-on-one protection. That was still me being overprotective like she had accused me of, but I couldn't help it. I loved that woman, and someone was threatening her, even though it didn't feel like a threat all the time. But because she was part of the family, she got one-on-one protection. She wasn't happy about it, but it did mean everybody got a rotation where they weren't doing tons of manual labor or dealing with assholes. In our line of work, we dealt with a lot of assholes.

According to Daisy and Jennifer, working with Phoebe was a breath of fresh air, and I didn't mind that. I would've liked to be working with her today, however, we were each other's distractions, and I knew that.

"You up for dinner tonight? Or are you hanging out with Phoebe again?" Kingston asked.

I frowned at my cousin. "Why did you say Phoebe's name like that?"

"No reason."

The door opened, saving Kingston from my response, and Hugh walked in.

"Hello, both of you, what's with the tension?" he asked as he set his things on this desk.

"Nothing, no tension here," Kingston replied, and I raised a brow at him. "You're just spending a lot of time with her, and I don't want you to get hurt if it goes south again. Not all relationships work out as perfectly as Hugh's. Though I will remind you that Hugh is on his second serious relationship."

I winced as Hugh glared. "I literally just walked in here and I'm getting flybys. Fuck you. And, I'll have you know that Daisy and I are endgame. Not that it's any of your fucking business. Though you are family, so I guess it is your business because all you fucking Montgomerys make sure it's your business."

"Hey, don't shoot the messenger. I'm just making sure that you have your head on straight. You guys broke up for a reason." Kingston glared. "Not that you told me that reason."

"We broke up because we weren't in the right headspace." I wasn't about to go into the fact that I was an asshole. They already knew that. "And hell, just be happy for me, okay? You like Phoebe."

"Of course I like Phoebe. But I like you more. You're family. You're my best friend. So fuck you."

"Fuck you."

"You guys are the sweetest people I've ever met," Kate said as she fanned her face, fake crying. "Seriously. My heart is just aflutter from the emotions going on between you. So adult."

"Sorry, Kate," I said with a wince.

"No. Don't feel bad. I like Phoebe, and I like that you're defending her."

"I'm not attacking Phoebe." Kingston threw his hands up. "I'm just making sure that you also spend time with me. Because I'm a jealous, jealous cousin. I miss my best friend." Kingston put his hand on his chest and stuck out his lip.

I tossed a crumpled piece of paper at him and he caught it, laughing. "I'm just making sure you are good. Sorry for being an asshole."

"It's okay. I'm used to you being an asshole."

"Seriously, the best family," Kate said, and Hugh sighed.

"And yet I'm joining them. They're very lucky that I love Daisy."

"You guys are adorable together." Kate winked at us before going back to work.

I glared at Kingston. Although, I couldn't be too upset about it. He was looking out for me. And I did need to get my head on straight.

We were taking things slow, slower than we had the first time. But I needed to make sure I was right for Phoebe.

I needed to make sure that she could trust me.

I needed to tell her I loved her.

It wouldn't be too bad.

Right?

"He stood on top of the railing on the second floor, naked as a jaybird, holding his little wee-wee, saying that he was a big boy now and he wanted to use the big boy potty himself."

I scowled at my mother as Phoebe threw her head back and laughed, kicking her feet. Allison, my younger sister, sat next to Phoebe, tears running down her cheeks even though the damn brat already knew this story.

"Luckily, he was holding onto the wall, so he didn't tumble headfirst off the railing," my dad added, scowling. "And then he pissed right off the railing onto the stairs.

Because of course he couldn't actually hold it, he just knew he didn't want to use a diaper anymore."

"Oh my God. Why didn't you ever tell me this story?" Phoebe asked as everyone laughed and I just shook my head.

"Why on earth would I have ever told you that story?" I scowled at my so-called loving family. "Why on earth would you ever tell anyone that story? That story was supposed to go to the grave."

"But you were so cute. You pretty much potty-trained yourself after that, though," my mother said, beaming at me. "Thankfully. Because this one refused to use the potty." She pointed at my sister, who looked at our mom with open shock on her face.

"Wait? Why are you telling Phoebe my potty-training stories? I'm not dating her."

She turned to my girlfriend. "Not that I don't adore you. But you're kind of taken."

We snacked on cheese and drank wine while I watched Phoebe immerse herself in my family, and I just let out a breath. I hadn't even realized I'd been nervous until this moment. My dad caught my eye and gestured towards the kitchen, and I followed him to help.

"What's up?" I asked.

"That's what I was going to ask you."

My father had met my mother in a parking lot. At

least, that was the running joke between them. He had been married before they met, and my mom had actually been friends with her. It hadn't worked out, though I knew there was a bigger story there. One they told me when I was old enough to understand, though it hadn't had a happy ending for some. But my parents had ended up stronger because of it.

They sometimes had game nights with my aunts on my mom's side, as well as with my dad's siblings. It was one huge Carr and Montgomery fest, and all of my cousins from both sides of the family sometimes joined in. At least the first cousins did. When you added more than that, it got too big for one house to contain.

But through it all, my parents had shown me exactly what being in love meant. And it hadn't been until Phoebe that I realized that's what I wanted too.

I needed to make sure I didn't fuck this up.

Only I had no idea how to do that.

"Your mind is going in a thousand different directions. Do you want to talk about it?"

"I don't want to screw this second chance up. I didn't even realize I needed one until it was in my hands and now I can't let it go."

"Your mom gave me a second chance once. And it was the best thing that ever happened to me. I not only got you two out of the deal, but I got the woman I loved. I really like Phoebe, Kane. She's a good woman, and I think she makes you a better man."

I frowned. "I wasn't a better man to begin with?" I asked.

"You could be the perfect guy, the greatest guy in the world, but when the person you love elevates you, it's worth it. I just hope I still do the same for your mother. And you can do that for Phoebe."

I helped Dad plate up the appetizer dinner we were having in the living room, and repeated, "I can't screw this up."

"Then work on it. The best advice I can ever give you is to talk."

"Phoebe's already amazing. What do I bring to this?" I asked.

In the next instant my dad's hands were on my face, making me look at him. "You bring everything. You're a good man. I raised a good man. Well, your mom did most of the work. but I helped." My lips twitched. "Phoebe sees the good in you. Believe in that. I like the two of you together. Be who you are. That's enough, Kane. You've always been enough."

I hugged my dad, knowing that I needed to hear that and hadn't even realized it.

I loved her. I had always loved her. But I didn't want to crowd her. I just needed to keep her safe. But in doing so, I would get overbearing, and I had done that before. I wouldn't do it again. So I had to find balance. I had to open up.

Which I wasn't good at. But I was getting better. At least, I hoped.

Chapter Eleven

Phoebe

In the weeks since the last note, somehow Kane and I had found our rhythm. We spent nights either at my apartment or his house, although we had been spending more and more time at his place because he had the space, and that way we weren't bothering Claire. Which was still a lot because we were trying to take it slow.

It was the odd sense of being safe when I was with him, even though we still didn't have answers. The fact that it had been so quiet and we were moving on with our lives should worry me, but it didn't. It was only in the back of my mind.

But today was all about cheese.

"The second message was all dick. All dick. No matter what I said, he just kept sending dick." Aria shuddered and I pressed my lips together, trying not to laugh. Aria's story was terrible, but the way she used her hands to explain the gherkin-sized image was too much.

"This is why I could never do a dating app," Claire said, sipping her wine.

I shuddered, reaching for my glass. "I'm so glad I have never had to use one." I frowned. "That sounds braggy."

Claire rolled her eyes. "Of course, it's braggy. You've got the sexy Montgomery." She drew out the word Montgomery, and I snorted.

"Excuse me, but considering you're talking about one of my cousins, I can't comment on that. But good on you for not having to use an app. Dating apps are terrible and I'm never doing them again. I'm just going to die alone. It's perfectly fine."

"You are beautiful, hilarious, and a talented artist. You could have anyone you want."

"That's really not true. Because everybody in my world remembers that my father is the amazing photographer, and I'm just his kid who happens to do the same thing."

"That's not true. You're just as talented as your dad. You don't have to compare the two of you."

Aria's father was Alexander Montgomery, a world-renowned and award-winning photographer. He had done large campaigns that netted the family enough so they would always be comfortable, but also more poignant ones that had touched the lives of millions. He was brilliant at what he did and used the pain of his own past in his work. I admired him and I knew Aria did as well, even if she bore the weight of expectations on her shoulders.

"I know I'm good, and I'm still learning. I don't need the pity party. We have cheese. What more do we need here?"

"Hear! Hear!" Claire said, and I laughed.

"I don't understand your addiction to cheese."

Aria shrugged. "It comes at birth. Sebastian could eat an entire cheddar cheese block and be perfectly fine. I need a little more variety."

Sebastian was Aria's twin and co-owned and operated Montgomery Ink Legacy, the tattoo shop. I loved how close everyone was. Kane worked next to the tattoo shop and Aria's art studio. While not all of the cousins worked in that building, enough of them did. I didn't work in the same place as my siblings, but I saw them often enough. In fact, I had dinner with them later tonight. This was just an appetizer, and I was only having a single glass of wine. Before too long Kane would be on his way to pick me up.

I was grateful for that. Though it was going to be a little weird to have him at another family function. For some reason we had decided to put our family functions back to back within the same ten-day period. It was as if we decided to go through that hurdle together, after so many months apart.

But there was no going back now, at least I didn't think so. It had been weeks since I had heard from the person that was trying to scare me, weeks since the shooting. Things felt stable. And that was probably when everything was going to explode, but I decided to ignore that.

"Where are you off to?" Claire asked, and I looked up at both of my friends who frowned at me.

"What? Nothing."

"You looked lost in thought. Are you sure you don't want to talk about it?" Aria asked.

"I'm just thinking about dinner tonight. I'm bringing Kane."

"Dinner with the family. I hear you had that with Uncle Dimitri and Aunt Thea." Aria beamed.

"Yes. And Allison was there too. Though I am surprised Kingston didn't show up."

Claire frowned. "But he's not Kane's brother. Right?"

"No, he's our cousin, but they act like brothers. It doesn't matter though, because we're all family."

"And you guys are taking over the world," Claire said begrudgingly.

Aria shrugged. "We're trying. Although Ford's brothers are catching up."

I frowned. "What do you mean by that?" I asked, thinking of Ford Cage, who was with Noah Montgomery Gallagher and Greer Cassidy. I didn't know him well, though he worked with Kane. But he was a nice guy, if a bit more growly and quieter than Kane was.

"Oh, they just had a few big business dealings that hit the news recently. And Noah and Daisy were giving Ford shit about it."

"Because family does that," Claire said with a laugh.

"You know it," Aria agreed.

"I'm sad Daisy isn't here right now," Aria said, and I nodded. "But she and Hugh finally have date night since Lucy is with Sebastian and Raven. It's nice that they're able to do things like that. But it does cut into girl time."

"I should feel bad that I'm leaving early to go to a family dinner with Kane I guess, since that also cuts into girl time."

"You should feel bad," Aria said at the same time as Claire, then they burst out laughing.

I rolled my eyes but leaned back into my chair. "This is nice. Thank you for bringing cheese."

"Of course. If I don't do it, no one else will do it right."

"That's not an egotistical Montgomery way of thinking at all," Claire grumbled, though her eyes danced with laughter.

"I can't help it." Aria's tone sobered for a moment as

she looked at me. "Any updates?" she asked, and I knew exactly what she was asking about. Things had been quiet long enough, and it worried all of us.

"None. There's no trace of him. And he stopped sending things. I want to believe it's over."

"Are they still going with you to your outside jobs?" Claire asked.

I bit my lip and shook my head. "No. They have other things to do, and since they wouldn't let me pay, it was just wasting their time and money. I'm as safe as I can be, with pepper spray and my phone on me at all times. But I can't live my life in a box, much to Kane's displeasure."

Aria grumbled. "I don't like it. Just like I don't like whoever tried to hurt my family is also on the run."

I glared. "I can't believe they haven't found him. Do you really think he flew to another country?"

"That's what the FBI is thinking," Aria answered. "It's ridiculous though that nobody can catch this guy. But with his connections and his old jobs, it makes sense."

"What old jobs?" Claire asked, out of the loop.

"The man who owned that other security company used to be a mercenary. He worked with some really bad people in the past and did some very questionable things. How he was able to set up a shell of a company that was supposed to be legitimate, I'll never know."

"Money talks, and he had a lot of it. Which is probably how he got out. Everything feels so unsettled," Aria added.

I nodded, feeling just the same.

"Well, hopefully we'll be able to move on. Which sounds trite, but I'm not sure what else there is to do right now other than hope the FBI can handle it."

They nodded and we discussed work a bit more, like the project I was currently working on that was a bachelor's pad to epic portions. He wanted it to look classy yet rugged, and I was making it work. Even though he made lewd jokes with his friends when they were there giving their opinions, he never made me feel weird or closed in. There had been a few clients in the past that thought because I was working on their house, *inside* their home, that I needed to decorate their bedroom.

Naked.

I hadn't told Kane those stories, but if I wanted him to be open and honest about his life, then maybe I should do the same. Only those stories were in the past, where I wanted them to stay.

"So, I was thinking about writing a book," Aria said out of nowhere.

I turned to her, my eyes wide. "A photography book?"

She shook her head, and Claire's eyes danced with laughter. So it seemed that my best friend knew what she was talking about. "No, I want to call it *Life,*

Liberty, and the Pursuit of the Montgomerys. Just add cheese."

Claire and I burst out laughing.

"Are you serious?"

"What? It'll be perfect. I'll teach you all the ins and outs of how to deal with loving a Montgomery. Because we take a lot of effort."

"So, you still haven't told him?" I asked, as Claire leaned forward on her seat.

Aria pressed her lips together and shook her head. Neither of us needed to mention who *him* was.

"Aria, I'm probably the worst person to say you should put yourself out there, but if it's killing you not to say something, maybe you should?"

She shook her head. "It would ruin everything. It's okay though. I have cheese. And this book idea. It'll make millions."

"It does seem like only a very small set of the community would appreciate it though," Claire added.

"I have 4,000 cousins. Add in that more than a few of us will probably end up in triads? Just think about the possibilities and the sheer number of people who will fall in love with a Montgomery."

"As long as they stay away from mine," I teased, and Aria beamed. "I really want to ask if it's serious and how things are going, but I know he's going to be here any minute. So how about you just blink twice if you're happy."

I blinked twice without even thinking, and she giggled, Claire joining in, but I saw the worry in their gazes.

Because I was worried too. Things felt good. They felt right.

So of course, they were going to blow up in my face at any moment.

When they left after we cleaned up, I was ready to see my family. At least, that's what I told myself. I loved my siblings, but I was annoyed that neither of my parents were going to be at this family dinner. Dad had some work thing, and Mom was out of town with her girlfriends and wouldn't be back until later tonight. They had both said they would come, and then backed out. But my eldest sister was great at making sure that we siblings stuck together no matter what.

Kane: *I'm stuck at a red light, and I'm pretty sure this means I'm going to end up hitting that train in between me and you. I don't want to be late, but I might be.*

I grinned at his text and picked up the phone.

Me: *You do realize that Isabella is going to blame one of us in perpetuity for this, right?*

Kane: *I love when you use words like perpetuity in a text. It's so fucking sexy.*

I rolled my eyes.

Me: *Vocabulary is getting you off?*

Kane: *I could eat you out on the kitchen counter again and get you off. But then I'd really want to shove my cock down your throat. I love the way your eyes water just a bit when I slide down the back of your throat when you relax. It feels amazing.*

My pussy clenched and I glared at the phone.

Me: *You better not be sexting while you are driving.*

Kane: *At a red light, though I think it's turning green soon. I seriously can't wait to taste that pretty cunt of yours.*

He ended the damn sext with a winking emoji, and I blushed so hard I knew that every time I looked over at him tonight during dinner I would think about him going down on me, and me choking on his dick. I hated that both of those ideas made me want to press my thighs together or ride his face.

Claire was at a work appointment for the evening, so the apartment would be empty once I left, so I closed up everything and waited for Kane to text me that he was downstairs. He had wanted to come up and get me, but that would've been a little too ridiculous considering we were just getting in the car right away. The security system looked clear, and the doorman hadn't let us know anyone was coming up, so I figured I was fine.

I locked up behind me and made my way downstairs. Kane was in the front of the building, getting out of the car as I came out, my dress swishing around my knees.

He looked me up and down and licked his lips. I nearly tripped over my feet.

"You look good enough to eat," he murmured as he leaned forward and pressed his lips to mine. Without thought, I wrapped my arms around his neck and deepened the kiss. When he put his hands on my waist, keeping me steady, I *fell*.

Not physically, but in every way that mattered.

I loved him so much. And this felt right. Right in a way that it hadn't before. We hadn't been ready, or at least I hadn't been. But this was different now. He spoke to me, he shared with me, and I didn't feel confined.

And it scared me like no other. But I had to be ready for it. I could be ready for anything.

"Such serious thoughts," he whispered, sliding his thumb between my brows.

"You're going to mess up my makeup," I teased, pulling back from him. I needed a moment to collect my thoughts.

"I'm sorry. I'm sure you can touch up that ugly hag of a face of yours on our way to your sister's house."

Mouth agape, I shoved at him as he laughed and followed him as he opened the door for me.

"I cannot believe you just said that."

"Well, if I said that you didn't need makeup, then you would say that you wore makeup because you wanted to. Or we'd start talking about the whole 'not like the other girls' motif that I know you hate. So, I'm going to call you an old hag. But you're my old hag."

He closed the door as I stared at him, shaking my head. I glared at him as he slid into the driver's seat.

"I hate that you can read my mind."

"I seriously can't read your mind, Phoebe. But I'm trying."

"You shouldn't have to read my mind with everything. I'm doing better about telling you what I'm thinking, right?"

"You are. And I hope I'm doing the same?" he asked, the uncertainty in his voice hurting me. But it wasn't his fault. We were both learning this whole relationship thing all over again. I leaned forward and brushed the lipstick off his lips with my thumb.

"We're doing good. Promise."

"Well, great. Glad we have that covered before we go to the gauntlet."

I rolled my eyes. "My siblings are not the gauntlet."

"Oh, I'm pretty sure they are. Will all of them be there?" he asked as we pulled out onto the street.

I nodded, even though I wasn't sure he could see me out of the corner of his eyes. "Yes. Though my parents won't be there."

"Considering I haven't even met your dad yet, I'm not surprised on that one. I am surprised about your mom though."

"I don't know what's up with her. She's usually at all of our family gatherings, but recently she's been doing her own thing. Which is great because that means maybe she's not pining over my dad. But I just feel like something's off."

"I don't know what it's like to have parents who have a relationship like theirs, considering my family is the epitome of nuclear. But I'm here if you need me."

"I know. And I'm grateful for that. And your family isn't too nuclear. I mean, I don't think the gold standard of the nuclear family of two parents and 2.5 kids really applies to a Montgomery."

"I suppose the number of piercings and tattoos really count us out."

"True. Did Allison decide where she was getting her Montgomery Iris?" I asked.

The Montgomerys each had a tattoo that was a family

crest of sorts. Even those who married into the family got it. It had been a running joke, as a brand to be part of the family, but people liked it. They integrated it into their other tattoos or they changed it just enough to make it theirs. It wasn't a stamp of ownership, but it was a claim in some way. Raven got hers after she married Sebastian, and had cried when she got it. Not because of pain, but because it was Sebastian who had inked it into her flesh.

Kane's was on his chest and intertwined with another tattoo over his rib cage, and it was like a search game in order to find it. I loved that, just like I loved that some people had it firmly on their forearms for all to see. His sister though had taken her time to decide if she even wanted one.

"I think so. She wants an entire rib tattoo done, and while that was the most painful thing I've ever had done, including getting shot, I think she can handle it."

"We're just going to gloss over the fact that you said you were shot because I don't want to even think about that," I said tightly and he reached over and squeezed my hand.

"Agreed."

"Allison can totally take the pain. Men are the crybabies when it comes to tattoos," I teased, and he grunted.

"That is true. We are babies. Kingston cried like a baby during his."

I laughed at the ribbing, even though Kingston wasn't here to defend himself.

Soon we were parking in front of my sister's house, and tension slid between my shoulders.

"Are you ready?" I asked.

He looked over at me. "Of course. I like your siblings. We can do this. We've done it before."

"You're right. This isn't a first time. It's a second time. I don't know why that seems more poignant."

He leaned forward and cupped my face, his thumb caressing my cheek. "You're okay. And I realize that I should be the one nervous right now, and I am because I know your siblings are going to kick my ass, but I don't mind."

"My siblings aren't evil."

"Of course not. But they love you and they're protective. I'm going to try not to growl back. Because I deserve the kicks."

"You don't though."

"I deserve the kicks because they love you. Not that either of us did anything wrong. They don't know what's going on between us, and we're figuring that out too." He leaned forward and kissed me softly.

The knock on the window nearly made me scream and I glared at my brother.

"Stop making out. Isabella says dinner is ready," Kyler said as I flipped him off, and we climbed out of the car.

"Jerk," I teased, before Kyler gripped me around the waist and spun me around.

Slightly dizzy, I put my hands on his shoulders. "Put me down."

"I feel like carrying you off into the house and locking this Montgomery out."

"My last name's Carr," Kane said with a laugh as he grabbed the bottle of wine that I hadn't noticed before now.

"You brought a gift?" I asked, grateful when Kyler set me down.

"Of course, I did. I am trying to schmooze your sister."

"Schmoozing doesn't work," Isabella said from the doorway as she was pushed aside and Emily ran towards us and threw her arms around me.

"It's been forever," Emily said with a laugh, and we danced in front of the house. I saw Sophia go over to Kane and hug him. Kyler did that fist bump thing that guys did, while Isabella kissed Kane on the cheek.

"We're not mean or scary," Isabella said as Emily moved away to hug Kane, and I went to hug my sisters.

"I know. This is just nerve wracking."

"Tell me about it," Sophia put in. "This is why I never bring dates."

"You get dates?" Kyler asked, before ducking Sophia's fist.

I found myself at Kane's side and we walked into my sister's house, laughter in the air.

"Okay, tonight we're going Italian. I was in the mood to make a bunch of sauce, so if you don't like it, starve," Isabella said and Kane snorted.

"I like the hospitality."

"Oh shush. I know your allergies, same as my sister's. And I really wanted ricotta. I could just shove my entire face in a bowl of ricotta right now."

I shuddered. "Really?"

"Hey, it's a type of cheese, I'll allow it," Kane said, and my lips twitched.

"Okay, now I'm a little worried," I teased.

"You should be," Isabella said. "Me and Kane getting along and agreeing? It's like hell has frozen over."

He wrapped his arm around her shoulder, and she leaned into him, her eyes bright. "I see this is the start of a beautiful friendship."

"We'll see. I need to keep my ice bitch image up if I want to get a promotion. So I'm going to practice on you, okay?"

He nodded, a smile playing on his face. "Whatever you need. Do you need me to act like the asshole or be subservient? We'll play this little drama for ya."

"Okay, I like him. I don't know why, but I do." My eldest sister smiled wide at me while Sophia went to open the wine and Emily brought out the bruschetta.

Isabella's phone buzzed and she looked down at it with a frown.

"Hey, it's Mom."

"You should yell at her for not being here," Emily said grumpily, as Kyler pulled her in for a hug.

Kane handed me a glass of wine, but my attention was on Isabella.

On the paleness of her face, the shaking of her hands. Kane had seen it too, his body at attention. His stance the way it was whenever he was on alert for any outside force. That was his training, not mine.

All I saw was the absolute despair in my sister's eyes.

She whispered something into the phone, but all I could hear was the buzzing in my ears.

When she set the phone on the counter, she looked at us, her mouth opening but no words came out.

"What is it, Isabella?" Kyler asked.

"It's Dad. He's dead."

The explosion I had been waiting for, the chasm beneath my feet finally opened.

And all I could hear was the screaming in my head.

Chapter Twelve

Phoebe

"Phoebe. I can go with you. You don't have to do this alone."

I heard Kane's words echo in my head, and I did my best not to pull away. It wasn't his fault that my dad was dead. It wasn't his fault that I felt as if I had no idea what I was doing. He had been wonderful, kind, and by my side for the last forty-eight hours as I came to terms with my dad's death.

And the fact that I hadn't spoken to him in weeks.

I wasn't even sure if I had told my father I loved him the last time we spoke.

He had been in my siblings' lives far more than mine. It was as if, as soon as I was born, he decided he was done. It didn't matter that I was so close to age in Emily that we had been best friends when we were little. When

I was born everything shifted. He no longer worked from home when he could, when he wasn't out on the road wheeling and dealing. He wasn't on the conference circuit.

He had basically left us, and my mother had raised us.

I didn't know my father. Maybe I should have. But I didn't.

My father had died, and I didn't have any words for my feelings. What words were there supposed to be? He was gone and there was no coming back from that. There were no second chances, or reconciliations. There would be no more time to tell him what I truly thought about him.

He hadn't even given us his name. We had our mother's last name, and I never truly understood why.

Then again, though my parents never married, Dad had always said he legally changed his name to her last name because he wanted their own version of a family.

"Phoebe?" Kane asked, his voice soft. He slid his fingers along my jaw again, tilting my head up so I could meet his gaze.

I loved when he did that. I loved him.

But it was hard for me to breathe.

"It's just a meeting. I don't know what it's about, but Isabella and Mom said that we had to go." I hid my resentment because I didn't want to go to this meeting.

I wanted to hug my boyfriend, to be with my family, and try to make sense of what I was feeling.

Because it didn't make any damn sense to me. How could I feel this pain for a man I did not know?

Why should I feel that way?

"I can go with you to the meeting. You don't have to be alone when you're there." He cursed under his breath. "I'm not saying this right. I'm not good at this, baby. But I'm here."

I sighed, that numbness that had settled in at my mother's phone call starting to ease a bit.

"I know you're here. I know. And I'm so grateful. But Isabella said it was only family. And I don't think she meant that in a cutting way," I clarified at the tightness in his gaze. "I just think that it's the lawyer thing."

Kane scowled. "I don't understand why you have a meeting before the funeral."

I pressed my lips together and shook my head. "I don't either. But it has to be done. My dad had a lot of business ties, and maybe this was part of his will? I don't know. Only Mom really knew him and all his business things. I didn't even see him often. What kind of daughter does that make me?" Pain started to slide through me, and I let out a soft sob, moving away so I could pace. "I don't know my dad's favorite color, or his favorite flavor of ice cream. I know that he liked the coconut flavored chocolates when we would get that sampler at Christmas, when he stayed for Christmas. He would always have something else to do that evening, because he used to say he had very important business. Because people relied on him at his company, and he needed to make sure his workers, wherever they were, had time with their families. So we would get him in the morning, but not in the evening. I know he loved this one sweatshirt with bleach stains on the cuffs. He would wear it all the time when he was at the house, teaching Kyler how to use a hammer. I remember he would sit next to Sophia and try to help her work on her pointe shoes and sew her ribbons on, but then Sophia would knock his hands away with a laugh and say she could do it on her own because she knew how to take care of her feet. Because that's what a ballerina did. They broke in their own pointe shoes. I remember him teaching Emily to ride a bike, while I followed behind with my little bike on training wheels, begging my daddy to teach me too. He said I wasn't old enough but he would teach me later. Only he never did. He forgot. Or he got busy. I don't remember. Isabella and Kyler taught me. I remember him sitting with Isabella and laughing and playing video games, and then going through her homework because she was so good at math that she was in an accelerated program. I remember all of this, but I don't remember him sitting with me. I don't remember anything about him with me. It was just always Mom and us. The six of us. And he would just sometimes show up. I can't even call myself a child of divorce because they were never married. Their relationship worked for the two of them, but never for us. And I'm so angry."

"You're allowed to be angry. You're allowed to be anything you need to be right now."

"I know that. Of course I know that. And you're being so kind and I hate that I'm so angry. I want to know why the heart attack had to take him when he was away. But he was always away. I want to know why Mom didn't call me. Why she called Isabella. Because Isabella is the strong one, my mom put all of that on Isabella to tell us, because she wasn't going to call us. Mom forgot that we were at Isabella's house. She put all of that on Isabella so Mom could deal with this."

"And Isabella was there for you. She held Emily and Sophia, just like you did."

Emily had let out a keening wail at Isabella's words. She had broken down into tears, and it was the first time I'd ever seen her do that. Even when Kyler had "accidentally" cut all the hair off her favorite Barbie, she hadn't cried that hard. Not that those two were equivalent, but it was the last time I had seen Emily cry nearly as hard. Sophia had stood stoically, her chin held high, her strong shoulders rolled back, and she had run her hand up and down Kyler's back, whispering to him that all would be okay. Even though it was a lie.

And Isabella had met my gaze and then Kane's, and I watched the pain in her eyes slide away, because she had to be the strong one.

I hated the word strong. But that was what we were going to have to be in order to breathe.

"I don't even know what this meeting is for. I don't want to go. Because if I go then it's over. I don't want to deal with the paperwork of death and meetings. I just want to hold my siblings and make sure they're okay. I want to be the strong one for once." My voice raised at the end and Kane just held me in silence, my strength, my pillar.

And I would have to be strong for them. I knew I did.

Only I couldn't breathe.

"You do what you need to, I'll be here."

I let Kane's words wash over me, and I knew they were what I needed.

He was what I needed.

I squeezed his hand, kissed his cheek, and let him drive me to the meeting across town.

It was in one of the beautiful high rises of Centennial, and I had never been inside this one before. I had been to Centennial, of course. Everyone in Denver had been to nearly every single suburb that was the vast sprawl of

Denver, Colorado. And if you needed to go to Parker or take I-70 down to I-25, you ended up through Centennial.

But I had never really spent time in this downtown-esque area.

It was beautiful in a glass-and-steel sort of way, but cold.

Perhaps there were other places in town that were much homier, but everything felt cold here.

Kane dropped me off at the front door and as I slid out, he reached for my hand again. "I'm going to wait in the parking lot."

"You don't have to do that. Someone will drive me home."

"I'm going to wait in the parking lot. Call if you need me."

I wanted to whisper that I loved him. But this wasn't the time. Not when I saw Sophia walking towards me, her eyes downcast, her hand tight over her bag.

"I'll come to you."

"You better." His lips twitched into a semblance of a smile, but it didn't reach his eyes.

Everything hurt, but we were doing better. We had to.

I closed the door and gripped Sophia's hand. She waved over her shoulder at Kane who drove towards the visitor parking lot.

"That's a good man."

I smiled over in his direction. "He is. The best."

"Does he know you love him?" she asked.

I shook my head. "No. I was going to tell him, and then, well, this."

I gestured towards the marble lobby, and Sophia sighed.

"You should tell him. We all need a little love I think."

"I love you," I said, and Sophia smiled.

"I love you too." My tall dancer sister leaned forward and kissed me on the top of the head. I rolled my eyes, a smile playing on my face as we met Isabella in the lobby. She looked as if she had been crying all night, but with her strategic makeup, only those who knew her could really tell.

"Mr. Winstone said we can head on back when we all get here. I don't really want to be here. Nor do I understand why we have to."

"Because it's in the papers," Mom said, and I didn't realize what I was doing until I ran towards her. My mother, all soft and warm, opened her arms for me and I clung to her. Tears threatened but I held them back. Kyler and Emily were behind Mother, having driven up with her, and I smiled at them, before sniffling once and squeezing my mom again.

"Let's get this over with?"

My mom looked at me and I couldn't read what was in her eyes. Did she know what this meeting was about?

No, I didn't think my mom would. But what could this be about?

We followed Isabella to Mr. Winstone's office and I looked around. "What are we doing here?" I asked, and Isabella shook her head.

"I don't know. But I have a bad feeling about this."

I slid my hand into hers, my heart racing.

Mr. Winstone was an older man with a shaved head, a goatee, and shrewd eyes. There was pity in them, and for some reason I didn't think it had anything to do with just my father dying. There was something he knew, and I was worried what it was.

"I'm glad you're all here. I know that this is an upsetting time, but per your father's will, this meeting has to take place before the funeral can occur."

"What are you talking about?" Isabella asked.

"Isabella, it's time," Mother said, and I froze, wondering what on earth she could be talking about.

Mr. Winstone sighed. "Come on and follow me. The others are already in the meeting room. They arrived just before you did."

My spine stiffened, as did my siblings'.

"Others?"

"You'll see." He gave my mother a pointed look as she walked past us, chin raised.

I was so confused, and this didn't make any sense. Isabella's hand was so tight on my fingers, I knew I might end up bruised.

But I followed Mother into the conference room, my siblings all around me, and couldn't believe what I was seeing.

The conference room was full.

The room was full of men. There was one woman with ice-blue eyes, and an even icier expression, but the rest were men with dark hair, narrowed eyes, and such similar features I knew they all had to be siblings.

However, as my heart raced, I realized their eyes were similar for another reason.

I knew those eyes.

Those were Kyler's eyes.

But no, that couldn't be right. Those were not my father's eyes. Not my brother's.

Everything started to crash into me, and my siblings began to mumble questions, confusion etched on their gazes again. The final person in the room who I hadn't recognized at first, stood up.

"Phoebe? What are you doing here?" Ford Cage asked as he walked over and gripped my hands.

"I was going to ask you the same question." I looked

into Ford's eyes, Kyler's eyes, and my mouth went dry. "We're here to meet the lawyer about my father's death, Ford. Why would you and the Cages be here?"

But things began to click into place. Things that made no sense.

Because while my father had taken my mother's name, each of us had the same middle name. The middle name he had said was his middle name.

Cage.

I was Phoebe Cage Dixon.

Ford staggered back, the other brother at the end of the table shot up demanding answers, and I nearly threw up.

"Phoebe, we're here from my dad's will reading. How? What the hell is going on?" Ford asked, and I looked around, my hands still in Ford's as everybody stared at us, then at our lawyers.

But it was the woman who had to be Ford's mother that spoke first.

"I don't know why you're acting so dramatic. You knew your father was an asshole. He just liked creating drama."

"Melanie, stop," my mom snapped right back, and I looked between them, my gorge rising as everyone continued to shout.

These two knew each other? No, this wasn't happening.

"We had a deal," Melanie Cage said, her voice laced with ice. "You would keep your family away from mine. We could share Lorne, but I got the name, I got the family. You got whatever else. But now it looks like Lorne decided to be an asshole again."

"What are you talking about?" Isabella asked, her hands fisted at her side.

"Excuse me, will someone please explain?" the one who had to be the eldest of Ford's brothers asked, and I tried to remember if I even knew his name.

"Well, I wasn't quite sure how this was going to work out," Mr. Winstone began, and everyone quieted, but no one sat except Ford's mother. She glared at my mother.

It seemed like I knew nobody here.

"Lorne Cage has certain provisions in his will for both of his families. And one of the many requirements that I will go over today is that this meeting must take place. Lorne Cage had two families. Seven sons with his wife, Melanie, and four daughters and a son with his mistress, Constance."

"We went by partner," my mother corrected, as if that was the one thing that needed clarification.

"Twelve?" Ford asked incredulously.

"Busy fucking man," one of the other Cages said, and I didn't know which. But apparently he was my brother.

None of this made sense. I had to be dreaming. Only I couldn't wake up.

I looked at my siblings, and then at the men on the other side of the table, and took a step back, and another, breaking my hold on Ford.

"I can't do this."

"Oh, stop overreacting," Melanie said, and my mother glared at the other woman.

"Do not talk to my daughter that way."

"It was always going to be an issue. All the secrets and the lies. And now the kids will have to deal with it. Because God forbid Lorne ever dealt with anything other than his own dick."

Everybody started shouting, and I just kept retreating, and then I was running through the doors, my heels clicking down the hallway. Ford called for me, and then Sophia told him to back off, both of them shouting at each other.

But I kept running, through the lobby, past the stairs and the odd looks, and out the front door.

Kane popped up out of the driver's seat as soon as he saw me running, and ran towards me, on alert from attack or danger.

I wanted to tell him that everything was okay, that I was safe. But it didn't feel like that.

Instead the crushing pressure on my chest ached, and it felt like a hammer was slamming into me over and over again.

But then Kane was there, holding me to him.

"What is it? What's wrong? Did someone hurt you?"

Someone did, but how could I explain that the man who hurt me was dead?

I tried to suck in air, and Kane looked over my shoulder at Ford, who had come running after me, and then Isabella who seemed to have chased him.

"What the hell is Ford doing here?"

"I—I don't even…" I tried to speak but couldn't.

Kane held me, whispering in my ear, "I've got you. I've got you. Are you safe?"

I nodded against him and gripped his shoulder, trying to let the panic attack slide away.

This couldn't be happening.

I needed to wake up from this nightmare.

My dad had a second family. Except I was pretty sure *we* were the second family.

We were the secrets.

And nothing was ever going to be the same again.

Chapter Thirteen

Kane

I held Phoebe to me and looked over her shoulder at Ford, confused as to why the other man was there. Then Phoebe's siblings started to follow. Why did they look so aghast and hurt? Then a couple of Ford's brothers walked out as well, and I wondered what the hell was going on.

"Kane. Jesus Christ." Ford ran his hands through his hair, his chest heaving, and I looked down at Phoebe.

"What's going on, babe? What happened?"

"Can we just go? I just, I think I just need to go."

I scowled at Ford. "What the hell happened? Who hurt her?"

"I'm pretty sure the same man who just fucked all of us over," Ford said softly, yet the steel in his tone worried me. Ford was one of my best friends and I trusted him with my life. Literally on some days. And something was wrong.

"It seems that dear old daddy had a secret family," Isabella said as she walked towards us, head held high. "I don't know if it's true, but from the look on our mothers' faces, it has to be." Flabbergasted, I pushed Phoebe's hair away from her face, as she finally started to breathe again.

"In and out. Just breathe for me, baby."

"I just. I can't deal with this right now."

"Then we're going." I looked over at Ford, then Isabella. "Does she need to be here for this?"

Isabella and Ford, followed by Aston, Ford's eldest brother, came over. They looked between the three of them and shook their heads. I wasn't sure how this was going to go, but I was grateful for that action.

"We'll handle it. And if we need to meet again later, we will." Isabella scowled at Ford and Aston. "Is that a problem?

"Not at all," Aston said, his voice cool, far too collected. "I want answers, so I'd rather not have the meeting canceled right now. But I'm also not going to force any of my...family to stay if they don't want to."

Phoebe turned in my arms, and I held her.

Ford let out a breath. "Family?" he whispered.

"Kane?"

"I know. Let's go."

I pulled Phoebe away as the three of them and a few other siblings began to talk over each other.

I got Phoebe in the car, and realized that one of Phoebe's sisters, as well as one of Ford's brothers, left at the same time we did.

Though of course, they were all siblings, weren't they? What the hell was going on?

As I drove back to my place, Phoebe finally took a deep breath.

"I can't believe I just had a damn panic attack. I don't get those. How weak am I?"

I nearly pulled over and scowled at her, but instead I reached over to grip her hand.

"There's nothing wrong with what you did. You want to tell me what happened?"

She laid out the meeting, and when she got to the part where both Ford's mother and her mother seemed to know each other and have some sort of deal, my other hand tightened on the steering wheel. "Are you fucking kidding me?"

"Not in the slightest. I wish this was all a joke. I thought I was there to grieve my dad, not have my world shattered."

"Let's get back to my place and figure something out. Or not talk about it at all if you don't want to."

"Ford is my brother? Oh my God, that makes Noah

and Greer my future in-laws." she whispered, her brain going in a thousand different directions. Mine was doing the same right then, and I just blinked, feeling a bit nauseous at this point.

"I don't have any words to say to that," I said after a moment, and then I was pulling into my garage and flipping the security system through its cycle.

As soon as we got into the house, I went into the kitchen and opened up a bottle of bourbon. She blinked at it and I shrugged before getting a couple glasses and two of my fancy skull-shaped ice cubes, and pouring us each two fingers of bourbon.

"I don't like it neat. I like it on the rocks. Plus I like skulls. Take it."

She took the glass from me and scowled. "I don't do this like a shot, do I?"

"No, you sip it. The burn will help."

She looked at me, then took a big gulp, wincing as she did. I winced right along with her as I took a sip of my own. It was a nice burn, but the caramel taste was perfect. I didn't like bourbon too smoky when I drank it like this. I only liked it smoky if I put it in an old-fashioned or some other drink.

"So, you're a bourbon drinker now?" she asked with a laugh. "Things do keep changing."

I shrugged and set my glass next to hers on the

counter. "One of the businessmen that I was a bodyguard for a while back drank bourbon. He actually had some stake in a few distilleries and sat me down once when I was off duty and showed me how to actually enjoy it. To breathe it in, to taste the different profiles. I'm not a fancy scotch guy who is going to enjoy a glass every night before or after dinner. Kingston and I are planning on doing the Bourbon Trail in Kentucky, where we go to a bunch of distilleries and taste bourbon and spend too much money. There's food involved too, so that should be fun. I don't know, but it's a hobby."

"It's a cool hobby. I don't mind bourbon. And I love old fashions. Especially with walnut bitters."

I grinned. "And here I thought you were a tequila girl."

"I'm a liquor girl." She paused. "That sounded far dirtier than I meant it."

I threw my head back and laughed, the tension beginning to ease out of me. Though not completely.

"I like learning new things about you every day." I sighed, not wanting to pry but knowing I needed to. Because she needed me to. "I'm sorry. About your dad. I can't even imagine."

"Of course you can't. Dimitri Carr is an amazing human who would never do anything like that to Thea. He is literally the epitome of the best dad around. He was always in your life. And now I hate that my voice keeps getting high-pitched." She put her hands over her face and screamed. I nudged her drink towards her and took a sip of my own.

"I'm sorry."

"Don't be. My dad had this whole secret life. I always thought he was a bad dad. I mean, I figured he sometimes maybe cheated on my mom. They weren't married, they were rarely together these days. I thought I would be sitting here mourning my father, not mourning the man I thought he was. I thought he was just an absentee dad. I didn't realize that he was a cruel monster who decided to have another family that he loved."

"He loved you," I said, knowing it was probably the wrong thing. "You said he did. I mean, he's a complete asshole, and I will burn his memory with you, but I don't want you to burn every single good thing there was."

"But now I'm not even sure there were any. We got Christmas mornings with him, but Ford and his brothers got the rest? Was he even in their lives? Ford clearly got the last name. Dad told us it was because his middle name was Cage. I didn't realize that even the last name I thought he had was a lie."

I fisted my hands at my sides, trying to remember everything Ford had ever said about his father—which wasn't much. I knew more about his brothers than his parents, and now I found that an immense oversight. "I don't know Ford's relationship with his dad, other than that it was a bit traumatic."

Her eyes widened. "What do you mean?"

"You should talk to him."

"How do I talk to him? He was just your friend, and someone I knew casually, but now what? We're related? We share a father. Or at least his DNA. Because there's no way that we shared a real dad. We didn't have the same relationship. Ford had one with him. I had nothing. And yet, I'm glad I didn't have anything. Because my siblings, they had more of a relationship with him. I had wisps of a ghost, and even those turned out to be a lie. And I just, I don't want to talk about it anymore. I don't want to think about it anymore. I hate that I'm running away from my problems but I don't want to talk about them right now."

I nodded and gestured towards her glass. "Good. Because we don't have to. Later we can burn down the world together if we have to. But you're not doing it alone. And I'm also not going to be the overprotective asshole who takes over." Although it was literally killing me not to do something about it. I wanted to pull up his documents and do every type of background check I possibly could.

I wondered if Ford was doing that right now. Maybe I would ask him later.

Hell, my business partner was my girlfriend's brother.

That wasn't complicated at all. But we Montgomerys liked making things super complicated, even though Montgomery was just my middle name, just like Cage was hers.

"I don't know if I could do this alone. And I really don't want to."

I looked at her, confused. "What do you mean?"

"I was so worried about figuring out who I was, but now I realize that I didn't even have all the parts in order to do that. But in the end it doesn't matter. Because I love you, Kane. And I shouldn't have pushed you away when I got scared before. I'm not going to do it again. I can't do it again. So if you need to back out because my family is now insane, and possibly larger than yours, just do it. But know that I will fight for you. I should have fought for you before. And I fucking love you."

It felt as if the world had crashed around me, and I was moving towards her, not even realizing I was doing it until I was. My hands were on her hips, pulling her towards me as I crushed my mouth to hers.

"I will fight for you until the end of the world and then further. I love you so much, Phoebe Cage Dixon," I whispered. "I've loved you for far longer than I care to admit."

"Oh really?" she asked, her eyes filling with tears. "Because I was such a coward in not knowing what it meant to love someone. I thought it meant that we had to have our lives together and our heads on straight, and it turns out we can be complete messes together and I'm perfectly fine with that."

She threw her head back and laughed until I kissed her again. "I love that you just called me a mess and I think I love you even more for it."

"You're a complete mess. But then again, so am I."

"I'll fight for you," I whispered again. "Always. And I'll protect you if you let me. I'll stand by your side. I'll do whatever you need. Just be patient while I try to figure that out."

"As long as you're patient with me as I figure that out too. I don't want to talk anymore though, Kane. I just want to feel. Is that okay? For now? There are so many things to talk about, but later. For right now I just want to feel."

In answer, I took her mouth and lifted her up off the floor. She wrapped her legs around my waist and kissed me as I carried her back to the bedroom.

Somehow I was able to catch my breath, to go slow, achingly slow. When I pulled off her shirt, I cupped her breasts in my hands, loving the way that they overfilled them.

"You're so beautiful."

"You make me feel beautiful."

I smiled softly before I kissed her again, and then

trailed my lips along her jaw, her neck, and down to the globes of her breasts. I undid the clasp of her bra and her breasts fell heavy into my hands. I suckled on her nipples, loving that they turned a dark pink, swollen from my attentions.

We lay on the bed together, stripping each other until we were naked, my hand between her legs playing with her folds as she squeezed my cock. She started to run her hand over my length, once, twice, and I let out a hushed breath, pulling away from her.

"I'm so fucking close and we've just begun," I teased, my lips along her earlobe.

"I swear I'm always wet when you're around."

"I'm going to have to start wearing different pants so I don't end up with a zipper scar on my cock."

She laughed, even though I heard the manic edge to it. I continued to kiss her and tried to pull us out of our worries and back into this moment.

Because I should have told this woman that I loved her long before this, but it didn't matter. We would have to look at the past soon enough, but for now it was just us. Just the present.

I slid down her body, pressing kisses to her flesh as I kept moving, and then my mouth was on her cunt, enjoying my feast. Her hands dug into my hair, pressing me closer to her pussy, and I continued to suck, to lick.

When she came, moaning my name with one hand in my hair, the other playing with her breasts, she was the most beautiful woman I had ever seen.

I slid up over her body again, positioned myself at her entrance, and slammed into her in one thrust, loving the shocked gasp that escaped from her lips.

"You always do that. You always surprise me."

"In the best ways possible," I teased as I began to move, rotating my hips at an angle to grind against her clit. She met me thrust for thrust, angle for angle, and when she came again around my cock, it took everything within me to will my orgasm away. Because then I pulled out and flipped her onto her stomach. I reached over her to my nightstand and pulled out my lube.

She turned in my arms at that moment, facing me. "I need you. All of you." She swallowed hard, running her hands up and down my lubed cock.

"I need you too," she whispered.

I kissed her hard on the mouth and then slid my cock between the globes of her ass, enjoying the way that her whole body shook as I did so. We had done this before, but I still took my time, gently easing her open with one finger, then two, using my mouth and fingers on her clit and pussy to keep her wet, on the edge. When I felt she was ready, and she pushed back towards me, I positioned my cock at her back entrance.

"Tell me when to stop."

"Just move. I need you. Claim me."

"You're mine, Phoebe. I'm going to fuck your ass and show you exactly whose you are. That this ass has only been mine. And it's never going to be anyone else's."

"Only yours. I promise. Now just fuck me."

I grinned at her words, loving how she got dirtier and dirtier the closer to the edge we got. I took my time, slowly breaching her entrance as she pushed back, letting out a low groan that matched mine. We took our time, easing into one another, and then she was coming again, face down on the bedspread, tears of joy and probably a sweet edge of pain sliding down her cheeks, as I pulled out and poured myself over her lower back.

A claim, a mark, all mine.

We both lay there, shaking, as I kissed her shoulder, letting out a deep breath.

And then she turned in my arms and cried, gut-wrenching sobs as she shook.

I kissed her forehead, then her cheeks, and carried her into the bathroom. I turned on the water not scalding hot, but to the temperature I knew she liked, and I cleaned both of us up and washed her hair. And when the tears were finally gone, I watched as she washed my body, bending down so she could wash my hair as well.

"I love you," she whispered again.

"I'm never going to get tired of hearing that."

"Good. Because I'm never going to stop saying it."

Finally clean and the water cooling, we got out of the shower and quickly dressed in comfortable clothing.

"My sisters and Kyler are probably going to be over here at any minute." Phoebe looked down at her phone and scowled. "Well, the group chat is active. But I don't think the rest of the world knows what's going on yet."

"Noah and Ford probably do. So it's going to spread around the rest of the Montgomerys soon."

She sighed and sat on the couch cross-legged with her phone in her hand. "If my siblings haven't already stopped by my house, they'll probably head here. You know that right?"

"That's fine. As long as they know that I'm not going to step out of the room unless you want me to. Because I'll still be the asshole to them. Not the overprotective one to you though."

"I wouldn't have it any other way," she said, scowling at her phone.

When my doorbell rang right after that, I met her gaze and nodded tightly.

"Text Claire, because I'm sure she's worried about you. I'll go see who it is."

I checked the video readout on my phone and winced, knowing that this was probably going to be a bad idea.

"It's Ford," I said softly.

"Oh. Well. I wonder if he's here to see me or you?" she said, trying to sound bright.

I shook my head, unsure, as I opened the front door.

Ford stood there, his eyes a little glassy and a little swollen.

"Hey," I said.

Ford let out a breath. "Hey. Noah and Greer were going to come too, but I told them I didn't want to overwhelm Phoebe."

"And you think Phoebe's here?" I asked, that bite of protectiveness and anger towards Ford's father leaking out.

One of my best friends in the world just raised a brow at me. "Yes. Are you going to let me in? Or did you forget the fact that we've known each other for years."

I sighed and took a step back. "Sorry.

"Don't be. This is awkward as hell. And I have no idea what I'm about to say." Ford looked past me at Phoebe, who had stood up from the couch, and came inside. She looked adorable, and so small in her gray yoga pants and sweatshirt. Her hair was wet and piled on the top of her head, and now I realized that maybe Ford wanted to be a big brother and to know my intentions. Hell. I had no idea what I was supposed to do in this situation, other than be there for Phoebe. And Ford.

Damn Lorne Cage.

"So."

Phoebe sighed. "So.

"I guess you're my sister?" he asked, then laughed. "I have no idea what I'm supposed to say here. Other than to tell you that Noah and Greer know what's going on, and I'm sure that the rest of the family will find out soon."

"That's what I said," I put in.

"But they're not going to tell anybody as of yet. However, this is going to leak into the media. My dad," Ford paused, and shook his head, "*our* dad had a lot of financial properties at stake. We're a potentially billion-dollar company, and so this is going to get out. Hence the meeting today."

I cursed under my breath, having forgotten that fact.

Phoebe frowned. "What do you mean? My dad was a salesman."

"He started that way. Now he owns—" Ford let out another breath, "he owned Cage Enterprises."

Phoebe's eyes widened and she staggered back. I moved towards her, gripping her hand. "Oh my God. I know that company. But I didn't know who owned it."

"Aston, my oldest brother, he's the one who runs it. A few of my other brothers work there too. I'm not part of it because I decided to start a business with this asshole and a few other friends," Ford said as he pointed towards me and I rolled my eyes, grateful for the levity.

"I don't know what I'm supposed to say. Or what we're supposed to do."

"I don't know either. There's going to be another meeting since the one today sort of dissolved. And a funeral." Ford pinched the bridge of his nose. "Because even with all this, Lorne Cage is dead and there needs to be a damn funeral. Although I'm not even sure that any of us want to go." He looked up at Phoebe and then at me. "I don't know who that man was to you, and I'm sorry. But you've known me for a while, Phoebe. So, well, I haven't changed. And I figured since we know each other, maybe we can be the ones to bridge our siblings together. Because I have a feeling that the drama's just beginning."

Phoebe walked over and reached out, gripping Ford's hand.

"Oh, the drama is totally just beginning. I have no idea what to think, especially about that man that called himself my father, but I don't want my siblings to get hurt." She let out a breath. "Any of them."

"Okay. So let's figure it out."

"I have bourbon, will that help?" I said into the silence that followed that statement.

"Yes, thank you," Phoebe and Ford said at the same

time and we all laughed, noticing that they each had the same crinkle around their eyes when they laughed.

This wasn't going to get any easier, but Phoebe wasn't going to be alone in it.

At least I could promise that.

Chapter Fourteen

Phoebe

Ford left soon after our decision to try to formulate a plan and deal with our emotions. Shortly after he left, my sister Isabella called, asking me to come to her house.

"We're going to have to meet with the lawyer and the other Cages later, but please come tonight?"

"Of course. I was going to call you."

"We were all hit with a shock, and I'm glad you went out of there." She laughed, even while I winced. "If you hadn't, then I would have, and I have to be the stone-cold bitch."

"You don't, you know."

She was silent for so long that I was afraid I had said something wrong.

"I think right now I might have to be. But we'll discuss

it later. Or at least tonight. You can bring Kane if you want."

I looked over at Kane, who was frowning at his phone.

"What's wrong?" I asked.

"Are you talking to me?" Isabella asked.

"No, sorry. One moment."

"I have to head into the office. One of the agents working on the case with Tim Sherman wants to meet with me. I can try to postpone him?"

I shook my head. "No. You go. I'll be at Isabella's with the rest. But you're invited, you know. You're welcome."

He kissed me, and Isabella sighed dramatically into the phone. I was grateful for her levity, because I knew tonight was going to be difficult. There wasn't going to be another way.

I shortly found myself at my sister's house, a glass of sparkling water in my hand, as I watched my siblings try to come to terms with our new reality that didn't seem all too real.

Kyler had a beer, but he wasn't drinking. He just played with the label, slowly picking at it until maybe something would make sense to him. As he set down the bottle, his fingers started to beat against the kitchen counter beside him, and I realized he was playing a melody that only he could hear.

I always knew that my brother wrote music

depending on his feelings and emotions. But now I realized that anything he wrote right now might be something I may never want to hear.

Because he was the only one who really got along with Dad, he was the only one of us that I thought might have known him.

Or perhaps that was just what I wanted to see.

Sophia stood looking out the window, not saying anything. Her beautiful dancer's legs were stiff as she went to her tiptoes and backed down again. She didn't go on point as she was barefoot, but she kept doing the motion, her hands folded over her chest as she stared into the nothingness.

Emily didn't say anything either. She just sat on the couch, her legs folded up to her chest with her eyes closed, tears streaking down her cheeks.

Isabella came out with a veggie tray and a pitcher of margaritas.

"Can you get the glasses?" she asked me, and I stood up quickly, glad to finally be able to do something. She had been in the kitchen when we all arrived and hadn't let us help. The fact that she had cut up veggies and made a ranch dip from scratch as well as margaritas without letting us enter the kitchen meant that she was focusing.

"So," Isabella said after I set the glasses down and we

all moved like robots trying to pour our drinks and crunch on vegetables.

"So," Kyler repeated, his eyes darkening.

"I have a spinach and chicken white sauce lasagna in the oven."

I blinked as I looked up my sister. "How did you make that so quickly?"

"I bought a rotisserie chicken from Costco and I slapped something together. It's probably not going to turn out great, but I don't care. It's fine."

"I'm sure it'll be wonderful," Sophia said, as she squeezed Isabella's shoulder. "You should have asked us for help."

Isabella just shook her head. "No. I needed to do something with my hands."

Kyler munched on a carrot stick and nodded. "Same. Thanks for dinner though. I won't stay long, I need to go, you know?"

I squeezed my brother's hand and let out a choppy breath.

"So, when are we going to talk about the giant pink elephant in the room? Because I think if we just break through that barrier, maybe we can freak out now rather than later. Because I already did the panic attack in public." Emily looked at me, her eyes full of anger even though her lips twitched.

Because that was my sister, she cried all the time, but it wasn't because she was using those tears as a weapon. She cried at commercials, she cried when she was happy, she cried when she was sad, and she cried when she was angry. No matter what she did, how hard she tried to hold them back, if she couldn't yell or fight back, she would cry, and that meant she was about to "cut a bitch," in her words.

Considering I had already cried myself out, I understood.

"I followed right along in your path. We made a great impression on the Cage brothers today sobbing in front of them."

"What kind of impression do we need to make?" Kyler asked, grumbling. "They're all rich, and they looked like they walked out of a GQ catalog. They're probably snotty assholes, wondering why the low-rung part of the family dared to be in the same room with them."

I scowled at my brother. "Hey. I know Ford and I like him. He's not like that. And in a weird twist of fate, I've actually met two of his brothers. Our brothers."

"Let's not give them labels yet," Isabella said. "We don't know if it's true."

I looked at her aghast. "You saw the way Mom was. And look, you saw their eyes. They have Kyler's eyes."

"Fuck that," Kyler grumbled.

"She's right though," Sophia put in. "There's no denying the genetics when Kyler is in the room with them. Although it's a little weird that you didn't notice before."

"A lot of guys have dark hair and light eyes," I said, defending myself. "It wasn't until they were standing next to each other that it all clicked. And what was I supposed to do? Ask the man who works with Kane who his father is and who his family is and why he looks like my brother? That wouldn't make any sense."

"No, and while you couldn't have given us a heads-up because you didn't know, it is a little weird that you have a connection to them."

I shook my head. "You obviously don't know the Montgomery family tree," I grumbled.

"What do the Montgomerys have to do with this?" Isabella asked, her voice steely.

She was scared. And hurting, and that's why she lashed out. When she finally let herself break, she would do it behind closed doors, and she wouldn't let us help.

Because that was my big sister.

It occurred to me that our mother wasn't there. I wondered if she'd even been invited. Probably, but I am sure she hadn't wanted to face us as a unit.

That was my mother.

So helpful.

"Ford is engaged to Noah Montgomery, who is Kane's cousin, and they all own Montgomery Security together. And the Montgomerys are a large family. They have a lot of friends, and a lot of spouses," I explained.

"So this Ford Cage owns a company with the guy you're dating?" Kyler asked.

"Yes. And Ford's a good person. I like him."

"And? What about him? Is he nice? What about his brothers? Did they know about us?" Emily asked, her words tumbling over each other.

"Yes, he's great. He's a little quiet, and I really only met him a few times, when I went to a couple of functions." I didn't mention that I had just seen him, because I needed a moment to think through that, and how I was going to explain to them that Ford and I were going to try to at least have the families meet halfway. Or at least meet at all at this point.

"And he didn't know?" Sophia asked, her voice soft.

"No. You saw how they all reacted. I think the moms knew though. That means we need to sit them down and figure out what the hell they were thinking."

"Well, I'm just glad that I'm on birth control," Sophia put in, and I blinked at the sudden change of subject and out of character statement from my sister.

"What?" Kyler asked, nearly spilling his beer.

"Dear old dad had twelve kids. I feel like that could be

a genetic fertility thing. I mean, the fact that Mom had five of us, and that other lady had seven kids? That's a lot of children. A lot of child support. No wonder dear old dad never married Mom."

"First off, ew," Kyler said. "Second, I think that would be bigamy."

"Hence why we didn't get dear old dad's last name."

"Yet he's labeled us anyway," Isabella added. "So, we're all Cages in some way. One big happy Cage family."

"I'm pretty sure the metaphor of us being lumped together couldn't be clearer," Emily grumbled, and I winced.

"When is the next meeting?" I paused. "With the lawyer, I mean."

"We have to set it, but I asked Aston," she said, her voice brittle when she spoke Ford's oldest brother's name. Or perhaps that was our oldest brother. This all was going to take a while to get used to. "Aston said we could work together to find a time that works. But it has to be before the funeral. Thankfully we cremated Dad so he's not sitting on a slab rotting."

I blanched as Emily ran out of the room covering her mouth.

Kyler scowled at Isabella before he went after Emily, and Sophia just shook her head.

"Isabella," I whispered.

Then Isabella stood and wiped her face. I hadn't even realized she had begun to cry. "I have no idea why I said that. That's the rudest fucking thing ever. Our dad is gone. He's dead. And somehow we're supposed to mourn him and we didn't even know him. I'm going to go apologize. I shouldn't have said that. You know me, I get into the analytical side of things and I have to worry about timing and now I'm just fucking things up. We're going to figure this out."

"It doesn't have to be us against them, you know," I said, my voice low, feeling for my sister.

Isabella shook her head. "I don't know if we're going to have much of a choice. I have a bad feeling about his will."

So did I, but I wasn't sure what to say. I watched my sister go as the buzzer went off for the lasagna and Sophia went to take it from the oven.

I wasn't sure how our family was going to fix this, or even if we could. But I knew we had to try.

Not for my dad, but for us.

It was late by the time we were done with dinner, and I texted Kane when I was done.

Kane: *I'm still finishing up at the office. Do you want me to meet you at your place?*

Me: *Do you mind if I meet you at the office instead? I don't think I want to go home yet. Claire's at the house, working on a big project.*

Kane: *I'll be here. Drive safe. I love you.*

I smiled softly as I looked down at the phone.

Me: *I love you too.*

"Heading to Kane's?" Kyler asked, his voice soft.

I looked at my brother and nodded. "Yes. Well, his office. I don't know whose house we're spending the night at."

"I'm glad. He's a good guy. I'm also glad I don't have to kick his ass, but I am going to have to kick yours."

I scowled. "Why? What did I do?"

"When were you going to tell us that you had a stalker?" he asked, his voice low.

I froze, looking at him. "How did you hear about that?"

"Ford mentioned it when we were in the parking lot. The others don't know, but you should have told them."

I pressed my lips together and shook my head.

"He hasn't contacted me in weeks. Kane's figuring it out."

"He'd better. Be safe. I love you, little sister. And I have a feeling that we're going to need all of our wits to deal with what's coming."

I nodded tightly and squeezed his hand.

"We'll figure it out."

"I sure hope so," he said softly. "Because we're family."

"Yes, we are."

I hugged him tightly and then headed to the office, grateful that I wasn't going to be alone. I wasn't sure I wanted to be for a long while. But I had Kane now. And we were finally trusting each other enough to lean on one another. I never wanted to be alone again.

He was waiting for me in the parking lot underneath the lights when I pulled in, an odd familiar feeling settling in. Thankfully he wasn't alone, Kingston and Ford were there.

I looked between them, frowning.

"Is something wrong?"

Kingston shook his head. "No, but I didn't like that this felt like déjà vu, so I didn't let him walk outside alone, and then Ford didn't let us walk outside alone so here we are. Your welcome party."

I laughed, though I was grateful that Kane hadn't been out in the parking lot by himself, and I didn't have to be either. The love of my life came forward and wrapped his arms around me and kissed me softly.

"How was dinner?" he asked.

"Complicated."

Ford cleared his throat. "Yes. Well, our dinner was complicated too," he said dryly.

I looked over at the man who was apparently my half-brother and shook my head. "Do you know what we're going to do?"

"No clue. But we're still friends, right? No matter what happens?"

"Yes. Of course."

"Good, because I would hate to have to kick your ass," Kane added, and Kingston snorted.

"Oh, the wild webs we weave. And I thought our family was complicated."

"Oh, yours still is, but then I'm marrying into your family. So now it's your problem too."

Kingston rolled his eyes and my lips twitched.

"I have no idea what my brothers are going to do, or your siblings, or what's going to happen in the future. But no matter what, we're going to figure it out. Nothing has to happen when it comes to those two sides. But considering you are currently dating my business partner, we're stuck in each other's lives no matter what."

I laughed, even though it was slightly hollow.

"It looks like it."

"And we're going to find your stalker." He paused as I froze. "Because no one hurts family."

I smiled then, giving an awkward laugh. "That is so weird."

"I know. Right?" Ford said, and the four of us headed into the office.

I felt like this was a new beginning.

At least I hoped it was.

I didn't know what was coming with my family, but we would weather it together.

Once we got through the trauma of learning that everything we had known was a lie.

I had my truth beside me.

In the end, maybe that was all that mattered.

At least I hoped.

Chapter Fifteen

Kane

I finished hooking up the camera, testing its Wi-Fi connection, and I tapped my screen on my readout, frowning at the source, and going back to fiddling with the angles.

"You almost done?" Kingston asked and I nodded, still frowning at the thing.

"Yeah, but I don't like this angle."

"We knew it was going to be a difficult one in the schematics. Do you need help?"

"I've almost got it. Then we can do a full reset and we should be ready to go."

"Sounds good. The customer's inside, I'll go talk with them."

"No problem. Let's get it done."

This was one of the boring parts of the job, but I liked

it. After everything that happened over the past few months, we needed boring. Something like setting up a security system for the small business that had vandalism issues in the past. They were across the street from a vampire café that our cousin Lake co-owned. It was one of those places that sold sangria and other red drinks in fake blood bags, and the whole place was vampire related. I had been a bit skeptical when I first heard about it, but now it was becoming a franchise within the city, and I had a feeling would continue outside of the state if Lake had anything to do with it.

Maybe I would bring Phoebe here later, as I figured she needed a little bit of a pick-me-up.

I didn't know what exactly was going to go on between her and her siblings. It wasn't really my place to know everything, but I knew they would figure it out.

Big things were on the line, things that surprised even me. I didn't even think Phoebe had really sat down with anyone other than Ford outside of her immediate family. Nor did I know if she had talked to her mother yet. Mostly because I hadn't seen her in two days. I'd had to go out of town, and Phoebe hadn't wanted to talk about her family that morning when we met for breakfast at my place. She had only wanted to talk about my trip and her upcoming project. And then we had gone down on each other because we could.

I fixed up the last of the angles that I wanted, and then got down off the ladder, fixing a few more things on the app before Kingston closed out the account and we headed back to the office.

"You still up for that gala tonight?" Kingston asked, and I sighed.

"Not really. But I'm there. It's part of the job."

"I know you'd rather be hanging out with Miss Phoebe."

My lips twitched. "Please call her Miss Phoebe to her face. I just want to see what she does."

"No, thank you. I accidentally called Claire 'Miss Claire' once, and I had to deal with that."

I glanced over at Kingston. "You seeing a lot of Claire?" I asked, a little curious. The first time Phoebe and I had dated, Kingston and Claire hung out a bit. I had thought maybe something would happen, but Kingston had started dating someone else, and Claire hadn't seemed interested. Then again, I'd had my head up my ass in more than a few ways during that, so it wasn't like I could really tell.

"What? Claire? No, she's like my baby sister."

I raised a brow. "I realize that our family tree goes through vast sections of this state, but Claire isn't actually related to us."

"No, but she's like Phoebe's sister, and I feel like

Phoebe is a little sister because she is with you. There's nothing there."

"Okay, if you say so."

"She's sweet. She really is. And she's funny. Sometimes you're allowed to just be friends with someone."

"That's true. And I like that you guys get along."

"Yeah, that would suck if I didn't get along with Phoebe or Claire, considering when we're not dealing with work, or things we haven't solved yet, we do hang out a lot." I scowled as we pulled into the parking lot.

"I don't like the fact that the guy left no trail. It's like he poofed."

"You're still not blaming yourself for that, are you?"

"Of course I am. I'm the one who talked shit to him. Then he put his little vendetta on us, and tried to take our contracts, and it turned into this."

"It's not your fault. You don't get to take responsibility for their actions, even if you feel like you should."

I ran my hand over my head. "Well, I can't help it. I'm a fucking Montgomery and a Carr. Of course I'm going to blame myself for what happened. But still. It was my fault at first."

My cousin glared at me. "Don't you go blaming yourself when we both know if I tried to do the same, you'd kick my ass. Don't make me kick *your* ass. I'm not in the mood."

"You're always in the mood to kick my ass," I said, trying to ease the tension since I felt like a shit for even bringing it up. I didn't need to put my burden on Kingston's shoulders. He had enough on himself as it was. If I thought I was bad when it came to holding blame, I was nothing when it came to Kingston and his own complex.

Hell, for a well-adjusted family, we sure had fucking issues.

"You know that if you pull this shit with Noah or Ford, they'd dress you down. It didn't matter that you might have been a cocky asshole for a freaking millisecond with that guy. He'd have gone off on anyone. It's in his nature. Not yours. And I don't think you were a cocky asshole, by the way. You were just being yourself."

I snorted despite myself. "That sounds like I was being one anyway."

Kingston's voice sobered. "We both know you're not, Kane. It's not your fault any of this happened. It's theirs. They're the one who hurt our family. They're the ones continuing to break the law and hurt people. It's not you. You keep trying to save everyone and keep forgetting to save part of yourself. Don't do that, okay? Don't make me, like I said before, kick your ass."

We sat there in silence as I tried to figure out what to say. The problem was that there wasn't anything to say. I might not have led us down this path, but I'd been part of it. There would always be could have beens and should have beens and I didn't have the answer to that. I didn't have anything. But I had to figure out how to make it stop.

All of it.

"So, you ready for your assignment tonight?" he asked, and I was grateful for the change of subject.

"Yeah, it's just three hours that I have to be in a suit and be a bodyguard for someone who doesn't really want us there."

It was part of the job, something our team did well. Gus had been scheduled to be on duty tonight, but he broke his leg falling down the stairs at another event the day before. Jennifer, his wife and partner, was beside herself over the accident. It was nobody's fault. Just a faulty step that ended with a broken bone. But that meant Gus was going to be on desk duty and cyber duty once he got back to work. Not that we needed him in anytime soon. It was good being the bosses so we could make sure our team actually rested. Though they, like the rest of us, didn't rest as much as they probably should.

"I'd handle it, but I have that other assignment across town."

"It's okay. It's part of the job. The fact that I haven't had to do too many overnights recently has been a blessing."

"And Phoebe knows the drill. Plus, you guys are in a better space."

"We are. I just don't like the fact that it's gotten so quiet."

"You know there's something wrong with us when I totally understand what you're talking about and agree with you."

"You're supposed to make me feel better."

"I will, but still, I don't like the fact that we haven't heard from Tim, or Phoebe's stalker."

Noah and Ford were in the office when we got back, Kate was on the phone up front, rolling her eyes at whoever was on the other line. I smiled at the woman, once again grateful she was there to handle that stuff so I didn't have to, then headed to my desk.

"Oh good, you're here. We got another call from the agent on our case," Noah grumbled.

I pinched the bridge of my nose. "Am I going to want to hear this before I have to go out on assignment and be attentive?"

"Now they're thinking he stayed in the US."

My head shot up as Kingston cursed under his breath.

"Are you fucking kidding me?"

"Nope. They don't have any documentation of him leaving the US. They had originally thought he used his contacts to get out of the country, but now they're thinking he's just laying low here. We were fifty-fifty on what he was doing anyway, but it annoys me that they spent time and resources on a trail that's completely cold."

"I don't like this lead weight on our shoulders when it comes to him."

"I don't either. But you know it's not your fault, right?" Noah put in.

I glared at my cousin. "What do you mean?"

Then I looked over at Kingston, who rolled his eyes and went back to his paperwork.

"It was never your fault. All of us have had to deal with the Sherman Group. All of us in this room and those out on assignment right now have had dealings with that man and other security branches who just haven't liked us. It's not your fault that Tim is a corrupt murderer. You work hard as hell and you need to learn to take a fucking break. And to give yourself a break."

"You say that, but he could have hurt Phoebe. He *did* hurt Daisy and Hugh."

"And we're going to catch him. I know that sounds trite, but we have to. We're keeping our family safe."

"Even if the trail runs cold multiple times on both of these cases," Ford put in.

I sighed, worried.

Because we hadn't found who had done this. We didn't know who had written weird notes and made calls and sent flowers to Phoebe. We didn't know where the man who had tried to kill us had fled to.

But there were things we did know. Like that I had a gala to go to tonight. And we had put up countless security systems in the last week, our business was doing well, and we were doing our best.

I just hated that it felt like I wasn't doing enough. That we were missing something.

I had just gotten Phoebe back, and I didn't want to make a mistake and end up losing her.

I tried to put that out of my mind as I focused on my paperwork, listened to my team around me as they worked, and tried to figure out where Tim could have gone.

And how the hell we were going to keep each other safe.

Except it felt like I was missing something.

Something big.

Chapter Sixteen

Phoebe

"**K**ane has that gala tonight, right?" Claire asked as she stirred the pasta sauce on the stove.

I nodded, my attention on the parmesan I was currently shredding. The last time I had used this particular shredder I had accidentally shredded my knuckles, so I was trying not to bleed into the cheese.

"So, he's going to be in a tux?" Claire asked, wiggling her brows.

I laughed, then nicked my knuckle on the damn shredder and took a step back. "Why do we have this thing? Don't we have a better one where I didn't almost bleed every time I used it?"

"We do. But the edge broke off and now it's sharp. I need to buy another one, so we are stuck with the one we had at our first apartment. The one we got at that Dollar Store."

I smiled softly, reminiscing. "Oh, yes. Our Dollar Store haul. I didn't realize you could spend $100 at a Dollar Store when you were supplying your first apartment."

"We did okay though. And we still use some of the things we got there. I mean, our serving dishes were Dollar Store gold for years."

"And now we're fancy adults. We use Walmart."

"I'll have you know that this serving spoon is from Target. I splurged."

I shook my head and went back to grating the cheese, happy to not be bleeding when I was done.

"What's next?" I asked, suddenly starving.

It had been a long day, and while I was happy to be done with my current project and ready to settle down on the next one, I also just wanted to relax with my best friend, watch a movie, and wait for Kane to come home.

Not that this was his home. We weren't living together, but we loved each other. We loved each other.

I still couldn't believe that I was in love, in a serious relationship, and was happy.

I hated how we had gotten back together, the reason that everything had shifted, but I loved Kane so much that everything else seemed worth it.

"You're thinking of him again, aren't you?"

"Maybe."

"Are you thinking about him in a tux?"

I had been thinking about Kane wearing only a towel, but now him in a tux where I could strip it off him? Oh, yes.

"Okay, get the dirty thoughts out of the way," Claire said. "You're literally blushing and it's heating up the whole room."

"I'm pretty sure that's your pasta sauce."

"Well, I made it from scratch. I really hope it doesn't taste like just sugar."

"How much sugar did you add to cut the acidity?" I asked.

"Just a little bit. That's what the recipe says. I've made this before, but I feel like it's different every time. It's not like Grandma used to make."

"Your grandmother was Irish," I teased.

"Yes, and she had a pasta sauce recipe that she was given from her neighbor, Nona."

"I like how the family recipe has been passed down through the neighborhood."

"I'm pretty sure the family recipe that was passed down through that particular family was Ragu, but I digress. Why don't you start cutting the bread so we can make garlic bread? And let's not broil it this time."

I cringed, remembering the fire alarm and the smoke filling the kitchen. "No, we'll do a little bit better than that."

"This is nice," Claire said after a moment as we began to work on the next phase of dinner. We were making a salad with pepperoncini and red onion—the full Olive Garden treatment.

"Eating dinner together?"

"I mean taking a moment for us. Between both of our jobs, and everything that happened over the past few months, we haven't had time to just hang out together."

I heard the wistfulness in her tone, and possibly something else, and I frowned. "Have I been a bad friend?"

Claire blinked up at me, wooden spoon in hand. "No. Not at all. I love you, crazy lady."

I rolled my eyes. "Thanks for that. Can we have a different nickname?"

"No. But I don't feel neglected or anything. I'm so happy that you're with Kane, if that's what you're worried about. You don't push me to the side or cancel our plans so you can hang out with your boyfriend. You guys love each other. We're adults. We live together because we like to, and frankly it's nice to be able to have a savings account because we're sharing the rent. But it's okay that you have a life outside of me. I will write in my burn book later about you, but that's just because I love you."

"You're saying that, but all the jokes that you're adding worry me." I set down my knife and went to her, holding out my arms. She rolled her eyes dramatically, set down her spoon, and hugged me right back.

"I love you, you fool. And I love you and Kane together. You guys were nice together the first time." She pulled back and went to stir the sauce and chop some more vegetables for the salad.

"That was nice, but there was still something off."

"Maybe. Or maybe that was what you both were thinking because you weren't ready. I don't know. I've never been in love or had a relationship." Claire winced. "That makes me sound amazing."

"No, it just makes you sound like you're waiting."

I was glad that she wasn't waiting for Kyler anymore, but I did want to see my best friend happy.

"Hey, I can see the way your mind is working. Don't do the whole thing where as soon as you fall in love, you have to make sure you set up everyone else in your life. I'm really okay. All I was saying was that I'm glad we're spending the evening together. While your boyfriend's out being all hot in a tux somewhere protecting his charge or whatever they call it."

"I love that you keep bringing up the fact that Kane is hot in a tux."

"I mean, he is. Do you guys ever play bodyguard?"

Claire held up both hands. "Pretend I didn't say that because I really don't want to know."

"Oh, maybe." I fluttered my eyelashes and she threw a crouton at me.

"I hate you and I love you. But please don't try to set me up. When I figure out what I want, I'll find them."

"Or they'll find you."

"No thank you. I would like to be the one in control."

"But sometimes it's fun when you're not," I teased and she grimaced, before we both started laughing.

I was just going to the fridge to get the butter when the power went out.

Claire cursed under her breath, turning off all the burners.

"Well, that sucks. I'm going to check the breaker."

"Yeah, that's so weird though. Why would the power go out?"

"I don't know. I wasn't expecting a storm."

Claire went to the laundry area where the breakers were, and I picked up my phone. I had no bars, and that confused me too. When the power went out, the cell service didn't go out. Unless there was something going on.

I looked out the window to see if the rest of the block was out, or if it was something worse, but all the other lights were on.

"That's so weird," Claire said. "The breakers are still on."

"Yeah, and the power isn't out anywhere else." I turned to her, and then I was tugged back violently, someone pulling at my hair.

"Phoebe!" Claire called out, but before I could even scream, a gloved hand went over my mouth and I staggered back.

All of my self-defense training went out the window and I panicked. I pulled at the man's hand, trying to tug it away, but then the moonlight hit the blade of the knife and I froze.

"Don't move. Don't move, little Phoebe. It's time to talk. And, Claire? If you come closer to me, I'll cut her. And I'll make it hurt. Go take a seat on the couch and we're going to have a long talk. Because I've been quiet long enough. And it's time you get to know me. It's time you stop ignoring me."

My pulse raced but I didn't move. I tried to remember what Kane had told me to do in this situation. Which was not what I was currently doing. Not to panic.

Claire stared at me, her eyes wide, and looked as if she wanted to do something, but with a knife in his hand, there was nothing she could do.

I didn't know that voice though. Did I? Who was this?

"Sit on the couch. Both of you. And I'm going to tell you a story."

He pushed at my shoulder and I staggered, falling into Claire as she caught me.

He forced me down on the couch and I gripped Claire's hand, both of us looking around for something, but the power was out and I couldn't reach a panic button. Kane and Kingston had placed them strategically around the apartment and my office, but I wasn't sure if it would work with the cell service out. This man, this man who seemed to be able to hide his IP address and where he was calling from, had turned off the cell service here. He had somehow blocked it.

Who was he?

The man came forward, the streetlight illuminating his face. He had dark eyes with straight black eyebrows and a firm jaw that looked like he needed to shave. His hair was pulled back in a tiny ponytail. He had on nice clothes, a black turtleneck, black slacks, and black boots, but they were worn at the edges. As if he had once been able to afford nice things but now couldn't. Who was he? How did he know me?

"You wouldn't stay away. I saw you, when you were with him. And he took everything. He took my business, and he took you before I even had a chance to have you. Why couldn't you see that we were meant to be?" he asked as he twirled his knife in his hand. That's when I realized that he also had a gun on his hip in a holster, and from the way that his pant leg was rucked up at the ankle, he had another there. Who the hell was this man?

"You don't remember meeting me, do you?" he asked, and I shook my head, bile filling my throat.

"I'm sorry, I don't. But you don't have to hold a knife on us. We can talk."

Claire squeezed my hand, probably wondering what the hell I was doing. Honestly, I was thinking the same.

"You don't need to try those things out on me. I used to teach people how to get out of situations like this. I was a hostage negotiator for my team. I forget though that you don't even know who I am. But your boyfriend does." When he grinned, I realized who this had to be. Everything started to click into place, even though it didn't make any sense.

"You're Tim Sherman," I choked out, and the man grinned. Such a manic grin that his eyes lit up.

"You do remember. We met that one time at that event when you were draping yourself all over Kane. It doesn't matter though, because our eyes met and I knew we had that chemistry. But I stayed away because I don't poach. I mean I poach other things, but I don't poach women. I'm a gentleman. And then the fucking Montgomerys and their ilk had to keep putting their noses where they didn't belong. They kept fucking with my business. And if you fuck with my business, you fuck with me. And then I have to blow you up. I didn't want to blow up Daisy. Twice. I kept trying, but I didn't really want it to happen. And then she survived, and my incompetent team members kept getting caught." He threw his hands up in the air, the knife still clutched in his fist, and rolled his eyes as if he were exhausted over the sheer stupidity of people.

My mind whirled and I kept my gaze darting around, trying to find a way to get to a panic button.

"I'm sorry."

"What are you sorry for? For not noticing me? That's fine. It's fine. I wanted to get you to come to me, but then what did you do when you got scared? Which, you shouldn't have been scared of me. I was just making sure you knew I was there for you when that fucking Montgomery or whatever he calls himself dumped your ass. But you ran right to him. You ran right to him when I was trying to take my final steps for getting rid of the Montgomerys once and for all. Why did you have to be in that parking lot, Phoebe? My Phoebe. It would've been safer if you were away. But you had to throw yourself into his arms, and I should have killed him right then, but I didn't. I've been waiting. Wooing you. But you keep going to him."

"I'm sorry. I didn't realize. But I realize now."

He grinned, even as Claire held onto my arm.

"What do you realize? Do you really think that you're getting out of this? Either of you. I mean, despair is what it is," he said, dismissing Claire and making my veins turn to ice. "But it took me weeks to finally cut through the intricacies of your electricity and everything else. The security system, oh, it was higher end, very complex. The Montgomerys have that working for them. But I'm better. I've always been better. I had to kill your neighbor in order to make that happen and move in so I could be next door, but that old man didn't really care. He was at the end of his life anyway."

Claire let out a shocked gasp, her hand going to her mouth as we both realized that he meant Mr. Jacobs.

He had killed Mr. Jacobs. The man with a kind smile who always held the door for us whenever our hands were full.

Tears stung my eyes, and then my head was slammed back into the couch as he slapped my face so hard I saw stars.

"Don't cry for him, you fucking bitch. You didn't see me until it was too late. No, we're going to have a little talk. I bided my time. I made them think that I wasn't a problem. But I'm their problem. I always have been. They took what I wanted in life, in business, and now in bed.

But I'm going to take what I want. It's mine. I'm tired of coming second best to the fucking Montgomerys. And I get what I want."

"Tim."

"Oh, you know my name now? So good for you." He moved, grabbing my neck.

I kicked at him and he slashed his knife along my forearm. Pain ricocheted up my body, as I screamed, Claire joining me.

"Get out. Get help," I called, and Claire moved to do so, but Tim squeezed my neck and threw me back at the couch then moved so quickly I didn't even realize what was happening until Claire let out a sucked gasp that didn't make any sense. And then there was this almost hollow sound of blade and flesh, as he stabbed once, twice into Claire's abdomen.

Blood welled and she hit the ground, no sound coming out from between her lips.

My throat bruised, I ran towards her and threw my body over her, trying to protect her from any more harm.

"Please stop. I'll do whatever you want. Just don't hurt her anymore."

I put pressure on the wound, listening as Claire's breath became choppy and her eyes widened.

"I've got you. I've got you," I whispered, hoping I wasn't lying to my best friend. But her blood pooled underneath my hands, in between my fingers. I had to stop the bleeding. I had to make it stop.

"I'll do whatever you want," I whispered. "Just let me save my friend."

"You'll do whatever I want no matter what," Tim warned.

As fear slammed into me, I realized that right under the table was the panic button, and he couldn't see me. So I reached out with a bloody finger and pressed it, and then quickly put my hands back over Claire's body, hoping that they would come. That Kane would come.

And hoping that they wouldn't be too late.

Chapter Seventeen

Kane

I was just finishing packing up for my trip to the other side of town when my phone buzzed, the computer buzzed, Kingston's phone buzzed, as did the alert on every other desk.

Pulse racing, I looked down at it, seeing that Phoebe had pressed her panic button.

Immediately going into protocol, even with bile rising in my throat, I called her cell. Then her landline we'd insisted she have installed. But when I heard an odd busy signal on both, telling me that her phone was either off or blocked, bile slid up my throat.

"I'm driving, you get in the car," Kingston said, grabbing his keys and anything else we might need.

Ford was right behind him, jaw tense, while Noah

picked up the phone. "I'm calling the authorities, and everyone else; you get there."

"On it," Kingston said, but Ford and I just gave each other a look.

The cops would be able to handle it. Letting them do their thing would be the right way to handle it.

We weren't going to do this the right way. We were going to do this our way.

"Call again."

I hadn't even realized my voice was so raspy until I spoke. Ford nodded and dialed.

Her voicemail.

Another call. Her voicemail.

Again.

Hands shaking, I sucked in a deep breath and found the calm that I needed all through my training. I couldn't protect her if I made a mistake. If my hands were shaking so much I couldn't stop that man.

"She's at the apartment, we're almost there. She lives on this side of town."

Thank God, I thought at Kingston's words, but I needed a moment to think.

"She wouldn't use her panic button for anything else? It wasn't an accidental touch?" Ford asked, and I glared at the other man.

"No. You installed some of them and you know her."

"I do. But I'm going through the motions right now because the woman I thought was just my friend who happens to be my sister is in trouble. Is Claire with her?" he asked, and then I finally got my brain into gear.

"I don't know. It was just the alert, no text. But she's in the apartment, which means whatever is happening is happening inside the house."

"And the alarm didn't go off," Kingston added as he drove like a bat out of hell, taking a turn far too quickly. I just hoped we didn't get pulled over on the way to her.

"How the hell do we not know anything about who this guy is?"

Ford reached out and gripped my shoulder, and I was grateful for the connection, even if I needed to scream.

"I don't know," he answered. "I don't like that this guy is trained. Or that he was silent for so long." Ford paused. "It is him, right? The guy who was sending her flowers. You don't think it's Tim?"

That thought had occurred to me, but the idea just made my blood chill. It couldn't be Tim. Because if it was, it would be my fault. Everything would be my fault.

Finally, we pulled up to the outside of the apartment complex, and the lights were on in most of the apartments, but not Phoebe's. Her drapes were drawn, except for one sliver, and it looked as if a flashlight was shining through and bouncing around.

"Fuck," I grumbled.

"Let's make it up the stairwell, just in case. Cops are on their way, and Noah said they know that we're on property."

"And what did they tell us? What are their instructions?" Ford asked dryly.

"Not sure. I hung up before I could hear them."

We were going to get in a shit ton of trouble, but I didn't care because Phoebe was in trouble.

We made our way up, and everything went silent. That pinprick of sensation that told me I needed to focus on what I was doing, because something was wrong and I needed to be alert.

I couldn't hear sirens yet, meaning the authorities weren't even close. It didn't matter. We needed to get to Phoebe.

A scream ripped through the hallway as we made our way to her floor, and we moved at once.

Kingston was breaking in through the door, gun drawn, and I followed, Ford right behind me.

The man on top of Phoebe had a knife out, his eyes glazed, and his hand over Phoebe's throat.

Blood pooled on the ground beneath Claire, but it looked as if she had moved to the wall herself, holding onto her stomach, her hands shaking.

She was going into shock, but was still breathing, and

Kingston dropped to his knees, putting pressure on the wound.

I could finally hear sirens in the distance, but I was focused on the man holding Phoebe, a knife at her throat.

"Tim."

"It took you long enough, Kane. Nobody can find me. Nobody did. And you didn't even realize I was the one calling your girlfriend. What kind of security specialist are you when you didn't realize what I could do? You had no clue. It didn't even occur to you. And yet you kept getting the big contracts."

I licked my suddenly dry lips and tried to remain calm, even as my gaze traveled over Phoebe in a quick motion. She looked bruised, a cut bleeding profusely on her arm, but it didn't look like she was hurt anywhere serious.

Her eyes were wide, but she looked calm. I knew that was just a facade, but at least she wasn't flailing, wasn't getting herself nicked with that knife.

I hoped she would do what I asked quickly.

Or all of this would be for naught.

"Tim, why don't you take a seat? We'll talk about this."

The other man laughed at Ford's words.

"You really think so? That's not how things work here. You guys don't even know what you're doing. You come bursting in here as if you have a right to be here, and yet all you can do is stand here and watch as I hold a knife to her throat. Do you really think you're going to be able to save her now? You were too slow before, and too stupid to realize what was right in front of you all along. You let the FBI handle it. You weren't even man enough to handle this on your own, like my team could have. No, you tried to follow the law, and now look at you, breaking down because your precious woman is hurt and you can't do a thing to stop me."

"We can talk this out, Tim. Anything you want."

The man laughed. "There isn't anything that I want from you." He raised his knife and I knew if I didn't move fast, all would be lost.

"Phoebe, down!" I called out, and Ford and I moved at once.

Ford dove at Phoebe, taking her to the ground and moving her out of the way as I took on Tim. I had wanted to be the one to hold Phoebe, but our training kicked in and Ford was closer. He went to stop the bleeding on Phoebe's arm, and to give me backup, while I dodged the first knife strike from Tim, then the next. The third sliced against my side but it was just a graze. I ignored the fiery burn as I took the man's wrist and twisted. He let out a sharp squeal and tried to punch me in the kidneys. I kicked out, knocked the man to the ground, and held both of his hands behind his back as he tried to kick out.

"Stop. Just stop."

"No. This isn't how it ends. This is not how I end."

"Yes, it really is."

And then Ford was there, taking over so I could hold Phoebe in my arms.

"Kane. You're hurt."

"You're hurt," I mumbled, searching her body for more cuts and bruises. Her neck was red, and already I could see bruises in the shape of that man's hands starting to show.

"I'll kill him."

"No, he's not worth it." Phoebe's eyes widened, and then she pulled away from me, running to the other side of the room.

"Claire."

"I'm fine," Claire rasped. "It's not as bad as it looks."

I met Kingston's gaze and had a feeling it was just as bad as it looked.

However, the sweet sound of sirens got louder, and I let out my breath, pulling Phoebe back into my arms.

Ford could handle Tim, I just held Phoebe, and waited for the pounding footsteps to reach us.

None of this made any sense.

But maybe it did.

Maybe it all clicked into place, just far too late.

Later, when we found ourselves at the hospital, Claire in surgery but looking as if she would pull through, I sat and let them clean my cut which fortunately didn't need stitches. Phoebe's arm did though, and as I watched the needle slide in and out of her skin thread by thread, I vowed I would find a way to make Tim pay.

"Stop it," Phoebe whispered.

"What?" I asked, scowling.

"You're blaming yourself, and you're probably thinking about doing something nasty to Tim."

The plastic surgeon doing the stitches snorted but didn't look up.

"I am not," I lied.

She reached out and gripped my hand.

"You could have died."

"I know. So could have Claire. But you did everything you could to make sure we were prepared, and we were. I am not a fighter, as is evidenced by the fact that I could not fight that guy off."

"He was a trained mercenary. You weren't going to be able to."

"But it felt like I should have been able to. It felt like I needed to do more. But I kept Claire alive. And she kept me alive. And then you came. And everything's fine. Everything's fine." When she burst into tears, the doctor pulled away and I held Phoebe close, keeping her arm still.

"Just hold on to me. Let the doctor finish his work and then we'll go home. I'm never going to let anything touch you again."

"We need to wait for Claire."

"We can. Kingston and your siblings are waiting too."

"What are we going to do, Kane? What's going to happen next?"

"We're going to get you cleaned up. And we're going to take you home. But you're safe now. Nothing can hurt you ever again."

We sat there in silence as the doctor finished up her stitches and gave us aftercare instructions. While we waited to be discharged, I sat next to her on the hospital bed, holding her close.

"I still can't believe he was able to do all of that. My poor neighbor."

My stomach fell at the reminder of the death that had occurred. "Did he have any family?" I asked, my voice gruff.

"No. But he was always nice to us." Phoebe wiped away tears.

"We'll make sure he's laid to rest. That everything that needs to be done is taken care of for him."

"I didn't doubt it for a second. If you didn't, Claire

and I would have." She let out a shaky breath. "Claire needs to be okay."

"She will be. It looked scarier than it was." I repeated the lie.

Phoebe looked like she wanted to say something, but Kingston walked into the room, his jeans still covered in blood.

I wanted to shield Phoebe from it, but she had lived it after all; shielding her wouldn't help.

"Claire's out of surgery. You're her power of attorney, so you can hear more about it, but the doctor said she pulled through. She'll be in the ICU overnight, and then you can talk to her tomorrow. I'm going to stay though, so she's not alone."

I looked at Kingston, gratitude in my gaze even though I wasn't sure what I was supposed to say. My cousin just gave me a nod and moved forward so he could lean down and kiss Phoebe on the forehead.

"Get some sleep. I'll keep watch over your best friend. You do have a hallway of family members out here, by the way. And not just the ones that you grew up with."

My eyes widened as Phoebe sat up and winced. "Who's out there?"

"Every single sibling you have. And your mom. Literally, all of Ford's brothers are out there. Nobody's talking, it's really weird. But, I have a feeling that things are about to get interesting."

At that, Kingston left and Isabella walked in.

"Don't, don't get up. I'm just checking on you. Then I'm going to kick everyone out and tell them they can see you at, I assume, Kane's home later."

Isabella moved forward and shifted so she could hug her sister.

"I'm really okay."

"We're going to talk about exactly what happened later. And you can decide how many of us show up at Kane's house, since apparently your apartment is a crime scene now." Isabella shuddered. "I'm really tired of our family going through things like this, okay? No more."

Phoebe smiled softly as I squeezed her hip.

"I promise I'll do my best."

Isabella met my gaze and smiled, the first real smile I had seen from her in a while. "Thank you. For saving my sister." I held out my arm.

"Come here." She rolled her eyes, but Phoebe's ice queen of a sister hugged me tightly, and promptly burst into tears.

That made Phoebe move, and Isabella and I both yelled at her to stop moving so she could rest, and that made us all laugh, and I held on to this moment, knowing it wasn't over. Not completely. We would have to talk to the authorities, we'd have to deal with Tim, with the apartment, with everything.

But the worst was over.

I mouthed the words "I love you" to Phoebe over Isabella's head and she mouthed them back.

I hadn't been able to protect the woman I loved completely, not from all harm, but now the worst was over.

And I wasn't going to make the mistake of letting go again.

This had been my second chance, and I hadn't realized it until it was nearly too late.

Later, as Phoebe fell asleep on my shoulder, both of us finally resting, I held on again.

She was my forever, my only, and I knew the world was waiting for us as soon as we opened our eyes again.

We would face that.

Together.

Once we took on the important business of life, and all of the consequences of our actions first. But it would be fine.

Because thankfully, we had our second chance.

Chapter Eighteen

Phoebe

I slid my hand into Kane's as we left the restaurant, my arm still bandaged underneath my blouse, Kane's shoulders sore from tackling my attacker. He landed on the same place that he had been grazed with a bullet after the shooting that began this entire adventure. While we were both sore, I was happy that we were on our own two feet, making our way out of a family meal.

"I'm stuffed," I said, leaning into Kane, feeling normal for the first time in a few days.

After we had left the hospital, I slept for a full sixteen hours, Kane by my side. He hadn't slept the entire time, but I didn't expect him to. The man rarely slept when he was on an adrenaline high, trying to keep me safe. And while that overprotectiveness might've bothered me in the past, now I understood it for what it was—love and trust. Trust in me, himself, and the situation.

Bad things happened, and we were figuring them out together, so of course I wasn't going to push him away.

Pushing him away like I had before might've been needed, but it was also pretty stupid.

"Me too. I can't believe how many nachos I ate. So many nachos."

We had been to a local sports bar because there was a game on, and the playoffs were soon.

A nice cold chill was in the air, and I knew Christmas would be here before we knew it.

I was excited for that, excited for presents and traditions, and making new traditions.

Kane and I didn't have holiday traditions yet, but we would find them.

Speaking of...

"So, are we picking up a tree from the store?" I asked.

"Considering both of us are allergic to real pine, yes. And they come pre-lit. Because while I can put up a security system where nobody can see it, I cannot string lights on a tree."

"And then we can use it year around. I'm okay with that. Real trees are great in theory, but all they do is create more work and break my skin out into hives."

"I've never had a tree before. I just usually go over to my parents' house," he said with a shrug.

"Claire and I have a small tree," I said, my voice slightly hollow. "It's in storage right now, but I'm still going to set it up at the apartment."

Kane met my gaze, and I knew he was thinking what I was. I didn't know if Claire and I were ever going back to that apartment. It was nice to think that I could be strong and overcome seeing my best friend's blood all over the floor and not have that burned into my memory for days and years. But the problem was, I did. I couldn't not think about it.

I wasn't sure what else I was supposed to do. Kane and I hadn't truly discussed it, I just brought things over to his house, and now I was there all the time. We would talk about it soon, I knew. But if I moved in with Kane, that meant not living with Claire. Which I also wasn't sure if I was ready to do. I wasn't sure if I was ready to leave my best friend alone.

She was invited to dinner with us tonight, but had wanted to stay in the hotel room, still recovering from surgery.

I shivered as I got into the car, then Kane pushed my hair back from my face. He stood in my open door and leaned down and brushed his lips against mine.

I loved this man with everything that I was. I loved

him so much it was hard to breathe sometimes. We'd almost lost each other, and I didn't want to think about that. Didn't want to think about the fact that his job was dangerous and it could happen again. But we were stronger. And I just had to believe in that.

"You know I have an extra room, if she wants to move in too."

I blinked. "Were you reading my mind? Or did I talk out loud?"

"No, but I had a feeling I knew where your thoughts went. I don't know if I want you going back to that apartment either. And I realize it's not my place to say anything, but I want you with me. Call me a caveman."

"I don't know if I want to go back either. And I like being by your side. Plus, I can keep an eye on you."

He raised a brow and I tickled his ribs. When he shimmied away, I laughed. "I could take care of you. I'm a little protective now."

"Yeah. You are." He kissed me again, and I sighed into him.

"Claire's not going to want to live with us." I bit my lip. "But I want to live with you. I do. I can't think of anything else that I want. Other than not wanting to leave my best friend behind."

Kane nodded. "Then we'll find someplace for Claire.

But it's taking everything within me now not to shout to the rooftops that you want to live with me. Because I'm really fucking excited about that, Phoebe."

I laughed, shaking my head. "I'm excited too. It's a big step. But I'm ready."

"You better be. Because I fucking love you."

"I fucking love you too," I repeated, using his same cadence so we both laughed.

"We have the meeting with the lawyer tomorrow," I said, knowing that bringing that up in the parking lot probably wasn't the best idea, but I felt safe with him standing next to me, liked that I could touch him while trying to sort through my thoughts.

"I'll be there. Just to annoy Ford."

"You love Ford."

"That's true. But you're going to need someone to lean on, and Ford's going to, too. If you guys are going to be the bridge for whatever's going to happen, I'll be one as well. I'm pretty good at it."

I smiled, hooking my finger in his belt loop so I could tug him closer. He gave me a Cheshire cat smile and kissed me softly on the mouth.

"We're going to figure it out. All twelve or thirteen of us. Or fifteen, if you include the moms?" I asked, shuddering. "That's too many people."

"Too many, but we'll all be there anyway. No matter what happens. Maybe something good will come out of it."

"Maybe. But I am relieved that we can even think about this and Claire without this huge weight on our shoulders. I still can't believe it was Tim who did all of that."

Kane scowled. "I can't either. But it makes sense in a way. He was trying to take everything from us, and we hadn't even realized he was a player on the field because he was so insignificant to us. Just goes to show you that we don't know what other people are thinking. We thought he was just a rival when it came to our business, and we worked hard to showcase who we were. And he lost his damn mind. If I keep thinking about it, I'll get angry, and we still have one more event tonight."

I raised a brow, my cheeks heating.

He rolled his eyes. "Okay, two events. I will totally make sweet, sweet love to you, or fuck you hard against the couch, whatever you'd like, but first we have dessert over at my parents' house."

"Please stop talking to my baby sister like that," Kyler said as he walked by, getting into his fancy sports car.

"I cannot believe you're driving that when it could snow tonight," I called out. "Drive carefully."

"I'm heading to the house, and I'll get into my nice SUV with my fancy tires from there. Don't worry, Mom."

"Oh, stop it. I'm allowed to worry."

My big brother glared at me. "We're all allowed to worry for each other. That's what we do. But do not ever say that sentence, the whole thing about what you're doing when you get back to Kane's house, because I don't want to know."

"Kyler!" I called out and he laughed while Kane just shook his head.

"I can't blame him. If anyone ever said that about my sister, I'd have to kill them, and that would be a whole thing."

"Again, with the overprotectiveness."

"You're not going to stop that part of me. Sorry. It's just who I am."

I loved that part of him. Even though it took me far too long to realize I could.

"So, dessert with the Montgomerys?"

"Is there going to be cheese?"

"Probably, though we do hold back for some meals."

And when he kissed me again, I wrapped my arms around his waist and ignored my brother honking his horn as he drove away.

"So, tonight dessert, tomorrow meetings with lawyers, but then the day after, what do you say we go for a hike?"

Kane blinked at me. "You want to go for a hike?"

"Okay, a walk. It's too cold to do anything else. But it's how we met. It makes me feel all warm and gooey to think about."

He leaned down and kissed me again, and I wanted to pull him into the car so we could figure out exactly how much of a contortionist I could be, but we were still in public.

"Later," he mumbled, seeing the look in my eye and I blushed hard.

"Anything you want, Phoebe. Anything. But first, cheese."

"I thought you said there might not be cheese."

"I'm a Montgomery and a Carr. I lied."

And with another kiss, he closed the door behind him, and went to get in the driver's side door.

Soon we were driving west, the dark outline of the mountains underneath moonlight filling our vision.

While things weren't completely settled, and we had a long way to go in terms of healing and figuring out next steps, we had each other.

We had family.

Maybe a little bigger than we expected, but we were all still there.

And I knew that what happened next, no matter who

we had to fight, metaphorically or physically, we wouldn't do it alone.

Because I fell in love with Kane Montgomery Carr long ago, and now I never had to let go.

And there was no way I even wanted to.

Chapter Nineteen

Claire

How were you supposed to know what your reflection was supposed to look like?

Was that truly what other people saw? Because the reflection of the woman in the mirror didn't look like me.

That reflection didn't even look like photos I had seen of myself on my phone or in an album.

That reflection looked like a ghost, their memory splashed on glass.

It was as if someone had taken the flash of a large camera and created a shadow that was suddenly who I was supposed to be.

I was not Claire in this moment.

I didn't know who I was.

I wore small volleyball shorts and a crop top, so I

could see the bruises on my thighs and arms from where I had fallen. Barely a stitch of clothing covered me as I lifted my arm up and ignored that it felt I was tearing my muscles apart from the inside out.

I could still feel the warm slice of metal digging into my flesh. As if the blade stabbed into silicone, that sucking sound when my flesh gave way and blood began to spurt, echoing in my ears. Though I wasn't sure stabbing through flesh made a sound. Maybe that was only the effect my brain had supplied so I could come to terms with the fact that I had been stabbed.

A man had stabbed me. A man who didn't know me other than who I was to my best friend, the woman who was part of my heart and practically a sister.

I had been in his way, emotionally, physically, spiritually. And because of that, he tried to kill me.

Or perhaps I wasn't a thing to be killed. He hadn't been in his right mind. Perhaps I wasn't a soul so I couldn't be killed. I was an object, far too nuanced to truly be tossed away like garbage, but not whole enough to be human.

He stabbed me, and I had seen the confusion in his gaze when it had happened. I wasn't sure that Phoebe had.

The man, the stranger, hadn't realized what that

moment meant until we were connected with his hand on the hilt, his knife buried deep inside me.

Now I stood here, countless stitches in my side. Not really countless; I knew exactly how many there were. I could count each thread on my skin underneath the bandage, though I couldn't count the ones deep inside.

I hadn't died, and yet the woman in the mirror wasn't me.

My hair was pulled back from my face so I looked gaunt and pale. I used to have a tan to my skin, a bronze hue that implied I spent too much time outdoors. But between my job and the fact that Phoebe, my hiking buddy despite the fact that she hated hiking, hadn't had time recently, I hadn't been outdoors enough. So my skin had already grown pale before the coming winter.

But the woman in the mirror had a gray tone. A gray of sadness and confusion. And the dark circles under her eyes weren't fooling anyone. No amount of color correcting and concealer were going to be able to hide that from Phoebe. Perhaps that was why I wasn't letting Phoebe see me.

She was safe with Kane, with her family that seemed to grow by leaps and bounds with each passing moment. She would be loved and cared for even in the hysteria that was her new family. I wasn't jealous because she deserved that. After the terror she had dealt with over these past months, she needed this. Needed to be with the man she loved, and to be with the ever-growing families that were the Cages, Dixons, and Montgomerys.

I didn't mind being left behind.

Because I couldn't let her see me like this.

I didn't want to be here anymore.

Not here in this world. No. I needed to fight. To survive. We had kicked and fought to survive against that man, and I wasn't going to take that for granted. But I couldn't stay in this hotel room anymore. I needed to go back to my apartment, I needed to pretend to be normal.

But I knew I couldn't stay in that apartment anymore.

My blood had stained the carpet, it probably stained the wood surrounding it.

And I would always hear Phoebe's scream, hear Kane shout for us as he protected us.

And though I knew they had fixed the door, I would still be able to see the shattered remains of splinters as it was kicked in.

Would they fix the blinds that had been torn when we had been knocked into the window?

Would they fix the chair that had been dented on the side, or the threads on the couch that had begun to unravel during the melee?

And even if they could fix the cosmetics of the apartment and change them for the better, they wouldn't be able to erase what happened.

I couldn't stay in that apartment anymore, and I would have to find somewhere else to go.

Somewhere without Phoebe because she wouldn't be coming back. And I was grateful. Not that I didn't love my best friend, but she needed to move on. To move in with Kane and find that happiness she had craved for so long. They were meant for each other in all ways.

But I would be alone.

Again.

My hand still held my shirt up so I could see the bandage and, lost in my thoughts, it took me a moment to realize I wasn't alone.

I didn't scream, though I should have. Instead, I looked into Kingston's eyes through the mirror.

He had circles under his eyes as well, and I wondered what they were from. Though I knew I didn't have the right to ask.

"Claire?"

I turned away, letting my hand drop. I didn't want him to see me like this. I had done so well in the little over a year that I had known him to not let him see me. Because if he saw me, he would know something that I couldn't let him see.

"Go away, Kingston. How did you even get in here?"

Should it worry me that though I still jumped at small noises, I hadn't jumped at all when it was him? Probably. I was probably in such a deep denial and psychosis that I couldn't focus on anything.

Or maybe it was just Kingston, and he made me nervous in other ways.

"I have a key. You gave it to me. Remember?"

He frowned as I met his gaze in the mirror, and I let out a breath.

"Go away, Kingston. Please?"

"You need to be resting," he countered.

I slid my robe over my shoulders, wanting to cover the bandage that he couldn't keep his eyes from. I didn't need to cover my body from him because he never saw me like that. I wasn't a woman in his eyes, just Claire.

"We're friends, Claire. Of course, I need to be here. To check on you."

I held back a snort, feeling angry for some reason. Why did he have to be here? Why did the one person that shouldn't be here have to show up?

Because I loved him. Or perhaps just loved the idea of him. I wanted him. I liked him. I admired him. But he only saw me like a little sister. And I wasn't sure I could be near him anymore and not feel rejected and broken.

So I would have to push him away. Because that overwhelming sense of guilt on his shoulders that Phoebe and

I had been hurt wasn't going to allow him to push off his white knight act and leave me be so I could mourn that woman in the mirror.

"Are we friends?" I asked, the words like glass shards down my throat.

Hurt crossed his features and I hated myself for it. But he would do better without me around him. He would do better when he didn't have the guilt over something that was completely out of his hands. It wasn't his fault that Kane had gotten hurt in the first place, or that Phoebe and I had been in the way of danger. None of it was, but Kingston Montgomery would always blame himself.

"Of course, we're friends."

I shook my head as I moved past him, careful not to touch him. Not that he would notice since he was always so careful not to touch me.

"Why are you here, Kingston?" I hadn't meant to let the hurt seep into my voice, and for some reason he reached out. His fingers barely brushed my shoulder and I flinched, trying to ignore the searing pain down my stomach as the movement pulled at my stitches.

He cursed under his breath. "Somebody has to be here, Claire. You shouldn't be alone."

I turned to him, holding back tears and just wanting this to all end. "It can't be you."

I hadn't meant for the words to come out, for the truth to seep into my waking memories.

"What do you mean by that?" he asked, his voice so soft.

"It can't...it can't be you. Please go. I'll lock the door behind you, but I need you to go." When my voice broke, he let his hand fall. Confusion splashed over his features, mixed with hurt. But he didn't say anything. He didn't fight. He didn't pronounce anything. He just opened his mouth, sighed, and turned.

His hand hovered over the doorknob for a moment, and I hoped he would turn and say something, anything.

The person I had once been screamed for me to say something. To tell him to come back and to hold her. That this wasn't us.

But that didn't make any sense. I was that person now. I was the only person. I was that reflection.

Kingston didn't turn. He left, the door closing quietly behind him. I went forward, my hands shaking for an instant before I forced them to still as I locked the door.

And then I let my hand slide down the door and I crumpled into a pile on my knees. My forehead pressed against the door, I finally let the tears fall.

Someone had taken my safety and my home.

Someone had hurt me. And everything still ached.

I was alone now. Where I needed to be. I could figure out exactly what to do about that.

And that meant I needed to be stronger. I needed to make a plan.

And I needed to get over Kingston Montgomery.

Bonus Epilogue

Kane

"But what if we run into a bear?"

My lips lifted into a small smile as we traversed the hiking path, that familiar question warmed my ears.

Considering I heard her ask that same question multiple times in the time we'd been together, I wasn't surprised to hear it now.

It would not be a hiking trip with the woman I loved without it. No matter how many hikes we had taken since we had been together, both times, she was always worried about seeing a bear.

Though considering the first time we met she had actually seen one, I didn't blame her for that concern.

"We talked to the rangers, and there haven't been any sightings in weeks." I squeezed her hand in reassurance, and she looked over her shoulder at me, narrowing her gaze.

"I know you're trying to be thoughtful, and yet I feel like you're making fun of me."

I shook my head, a smile still playing on my face. "I promise I'm not. But don't worry, if there is a bear, I will push you down and run away. Because we both know it's not the bear you have to be worried about, it's the person who's faster than you."

She pushed at my hip, laughing. "Jerk."

I grinned. "What? Don't you want me to be safe? You love me. I mean, it makes sense that you would want me to survive a bear attack."

"And then you just, what, leave me behind?" she asked, shaking her head. "I see. I love you enough to be mauled by a bear to protect you."

"There. I knew you'd understand. I just have to be faster than you."

"Well, you wouldn't even have to push me down for that. I'd trip all on my own."

She pointed down to her muddy knee and I winced. We had started off our hike like we always did, eating a granola bar, watching the sun rise, and then three steps later, she took a tumble. I caught her so she hadn't actually hurt herself, but she still somehow ended up with mud on her knee. I wasn't sure how that happened, but we were used to it at this point. It was just Phoebe.

"I've had a tough day."

"I'll say. You got coffee in bed, a Danish, a granola bar, and then you nearly fell flat on your face."

"I feel like I need to kick you. But then I'd probably fall."

"True. And you don't want the bear to get you." I reached out, tickling her sides, as she laughed and ran up the hill. I followed her, keeping an eye on our surroundings. Just because I was teasing her about a bear, didn't mean I wasn't actually on the lookout for one.

"How much further?" she asked, and I squeezed her hands as we made our way down around a curve.

"Not too much further. We're going to that picnic space you like, right? The one that you and Claire go to."

She nodded, taking a deep breath as we continued to walk. The scent of the forest was gorgeous. Crisp, clean, and probably going to hit our allergies later, but it was totally worth it. Today was going to be totally worth it. If I didn't throw up and get stressed out. But then again, today was nothing. In terms of stress levels, in terms of anxiety and danger, today was literally a walk in the park. We had been through hell together, had seen the worst in humanity, and had come out stronger because of it.

So today wasn't all bad. It wasn't going to be an ending.

That was, as long as I didn't let the stress of what I was about to do ruin everything. Because I felt like it could be a possibility if I didn't get my act together.

I didn't have backup for this, Kingston wasn't going to be at my side, ready to take over if I failed.

This was it. There was literally no coming back from this.

And I couldn't wait.

"Here it is. Oh, they took out a few of the benches. That's sad."

I frowned and looked around the area, annoyed that the bench that I had been picturing was no longer there. In fact, most of the benches were gone.

I did a full circle, taking in my surroundings again, and scowled.

"They didn't get all of it," I grumbled as Phoebe came to my side.

"What?"

"It looks like there was some vandalism. There's part of a bench over there, with graffiti on it and what look like some burn marks."

"How horrible. This place was always so gorgeous. Yes, they were manmade benches, but it was always set back so it looked as if it were truly part of the scenery.

Nothing too much or too out of place. And someone ruined it. How could they ruin this area?"

I pulled her into my arms, rethinking my plans. This wasn't exactly the mood I was going for.

"I'm sorry, babe. We can talk to the rangers though, see if there's something we can do."

"It's state-funded though, do you think they can really let us do anything to help?"

"They might." I frowned, a few new plans formulating. I wasn't the person to talk to about this. If anything, one of my other cousins who worked in construction, or even Lake, who had connections everywhere, could help.

"We'll talk to Lake and a few of the cousins." I paused. "We can talk to one of your brothers. They might know what to do, too."

She stiffened for a moment before relaxing marginally. This was our reality now, what we were going into in the future. Perhaps me bringing up topics better left unsaid would be better for everybody? Or maybe I just had my foot in my mouth.

"You're right. Maybe Aston can help. He rules the world or something."

My lips twitched. "I don't think Aston could do that. Although, if you ask Ford, that's the truth."

Phoebe grinned. "I still can't believe Ford is my brother. That is just so weird."

"Considering he's like a cousin-in-law, I don't know how that makes you and I related."

"We've already gone over this. We are not looking into the family tree. Things get scary when you shake things out of them."

I laughed, squeezing her close.

"I'm sorry the benches are gone. But there's an old stump over there. Do you want to go sit down and have our snack? Then we can head back. I know the real world is waiting."

As was Kingston, because the damn man was nosy as hell and needed answers.

Didn't we all.

"I was so excited to sit out here, in the same place that we always do. Claire fell face-first in the mud over there, and then I did the same right after I laughed at her for it."

I shook my head. "The number of times you two fall on hikes, why do you even do them? Maybe we should just sit down comfortably and do nothing."

"Thank you. I would love to be a video gamer. Is there something I can do that's super easy? Maybe like Sims or something."

"Sims is not good for your blood pressure. Neither is Mario Kart."

She shuddered. "We're not going to discuss Mario Kart. I cannot believe you hit me with a blue shell."

I shook my head. "I shouldn't have brought it up." Especially not today.

"No, you shouldn't have. But it's okay. I love you anyway."

Hearing her say those words still did something to me. I could barely hold back. I couldn't believe that this woman loved me. That I was lucky enough to have her love me.

We had both made mistakes, both screwed up things more than once, and yet she was everything. My everything. In the end I knew who I wanted to do this with.

We didn't need park benches or the memories of days past.

We just needed now.

Something crunched behind us and Phoebe whirled. I put her behind me, narrowing my gaze. When two deer walked past, crunching along the undergrowth, I relaxed, and Phoebe began to shake behind me, laughter bursting from her lips.

"I really thought that would be a bear."

I smiled down at her and turned. "You know, same."

She punched me in the shoulder. "Are you serious? You were the one that said there were no bears."

"I'm never going to lie to you. There might be bears. But I'll protect you. I promise I won't run away without you. Or push you down."

"Because I'll fall on my own?" she added sarcastically.

I shrugged. "You're the one who said it."

"You're such a jerk. But I love you."

"I love you too, Phoebe. Always."

And as she laughed again, I went down to one knee. This hadn't been how I planned on doing this, wasn't quite sure what I was supposed to say next, but she stopped speaking immediately, her eyes going wide.

I could hear other people coming up the trail, their voices echoing, but I ignored them. A thousand people could watch us do this, but in my mind, in this moment, it was just the two of us. We were all alone and that's all that mattered.

"Phoebe. I will forever love the day that you got into my car without knowing who I was. Wondering if I was a serial killer."

She blushed so prettily but didn't say anything.

"I have loved you for so long it's hard for me to remember exactly when that moment happened. But all I know is that my life is brighter with you. My future is brighter with you. I know that we both found out who we could be together over time, and I love that we're going to constantly figure out what that means."

"I love you, Phoebe Cage Dixon. And I will love you until the end of our days. Please make me a very happy man and marry me. And help us blend our families together again, so that we confuse everybody who's not one of us and scare the world."

She threw her head back and laughed. "Did you just ask me to marry you so we can form a conglomerate and take over the world?"

"Well, it seemed as good a reason as any. Of course, me loving you is probably the best reason."

"I love you so much, Kane. Of course, I'll marry you. But that does make me a Cage Dixon Montgomery."

"We'll add it to the letterhead. I promise."

My heart burst, my hands shaking, and when I pulled the ring out of my pocket, tears trailed down her face and she held out her hand.

"You make me so happy, Phoebe. Even when I know we annoy the fuck out of each other."

She laughed again. "Of course, I have to annoy you. It's my love language."

I slid the ring on her finger, a small decently sized oval diamond that glittered in the sunlight. I heard cheers around us but I ignored the strangers and stood up, pressing my lips to hers.

"Congratulations!" someone called out and we froze, then realized that those were familiar voices.

I turned, Phoebe still in my arms, as Kingston stood there, waving with one hand, his phone in the other, apparently recording.

Ford, Noah, Greer, Brooke, Leif, Lake, Nick, Sebastian, Raven, Daisy, Hugh, Claire, Leo, May, Gus, Jennifer, Kate, and Sawyer all stood there, hidden in the trees, laughing and cheering along.

How the seemingly 100 of them stood there without making a sound before now made me question my own existence and training.

"How the hell are you guys all here?" I growled.

Kingston, the ringleader of course, beamed. "The people with actual security skills who knew how to be quiet were up front, the rest trailed behind. Thankfully you guys stood up here long enough that we were able to catch up."

"I'm never hiking again," Kate called out, and I laughed, Phoebe giggling at my side.

"Well, this is ridiculous. But, she said yes."

Phoebe held out her hand. "I said yes!"

And then the Montgomerys, and the team, fell upon us, and somehow I was being hugged, kissed, and had my back slapped.

I laughed, taking it all in. And when I looked over at Phoebe, she gave me a look.

"This is what you're marrying into."

"Just wait until you see my family learn the news."

Ford had his arm around her, laughing. "Oh, they already know. And you're lucky they aren't here."

"It's why I recorded it!" Kingston put in.

"Well hell, this wedding's going to have 2,000 people already," I grumbled, but then I beamed, having Phoebe in my arms again.

"Let's elope?" she asked.

When everyone complained, I pressed my lips to hers and sighed.

"That sounds like a plan."

Only I had a feeling the Montgomerys and the Cages and the Carrs might not let that happen.

Or maybe we wouldn't give them a choice.

Because Phoebe was mine. Forever and always.

And my second chance.

NEXT IN THE MONTGOMERY INK LEGACY SERIES:
Kingston & Claire change the game in ONE NIGHT WITH YOU.

A Note from Carrie Ann Ryan

Thank you so much for reading **HIS SECOND CHANCE!**

I've been wanting to write this book for YEARS and I finally figured out how to get it done lol. That first scene was actually based on a true story, though with a mountain lion vs a bear. There might have been blacking out haha.

The next book in the series is Kingston and Claire's romance and oooof. They surprised me and I cannot wait for you to read One Night with You!

And as for Ford and Phoebe's siblings? Yes! Their series will be called The Cage Family with book one, The Forever Rule featuring Ford's eldest brother, Aston!

BTW Greer's brothers get their own series called the First Time series. Heath will be book 1 in Good Time

Boyfriend!! Three brothers. Three books. And all the emotional heat. Because the Cassidy brothers are

The Montgomery Ink Legacy Series:

Book 1: Bittersweet Promises
Book 2: At First Meet
Book 2.5: Happily Ever Never
Book 3: Longtime Crush
Book 4: Best Friend Temptation
Book 4.5: Happily Ever Maybe
Book 5: Last First Kiss
Book 6: His Second Chance
Book 7: One Night with You

**IF YOU'D LIKE TO READ A BONUS SCENE FROM DAISY &
HUGH:
CHECK OUT THIS SPECIAL EPILOGUE!**

NEXT IN THE MONTGOMERY INK LEGACY SERIES:

**Kingston & Claire change the game in ONE
NIGHT WITH YOU.**

If you want to make sure you know what's coming next from me, you can sign up for my newsletter at www. CarrieAnnRyan.com; follow me on twitter at

@CarrieAnnRyan, or like my Facebook page. I also have a Facebook Fan Club where we have trivia, chats, and other goodies. You guys are the reason I get to do what I do and I thank you.

Make sure you're signed up for my MAILING LIST so you can know when the next releases are available as well as find giveaways and FREE READS.

Happy Reading!

Also from Carrie Ann Ryan

The Montgomery Ink Legacy Series:

Book 1: Bittersweet Promises (Leif & Brooke)

Book 2: At First Meet (Nick & Lake)

Book 2.5: Happily Ever Never (May & Leo)

Book 3: Longtime Crush (Sebastian & Raven)

Book 4: Best Friend Temptation (Noah, Ford, and Greer)

Book 4.5: Happily Ever Maybe (Jennifer & Gus)

Book 5: Last First Kiss (Daisy & Hugh)

Book 6: His Second Chance (Kane & Phoebe)

Book 7: One Night with You (Kingston & Claire)

The Wilder Brothers Series:

Book 1: One Way Back to Me (Eli & Alexis)

Book 2: Always the One for Me (Evan & Kendall)

Book 3: The Path to You (Everett & Bethany)

Book 4: Coming Home for Us (Elijah & Maddie)

Book 5: Stay Here With Me (East & Lark)

Book 6: Finding the Road to Us (Elliot, Trace, and Sidney)

Book 7: Moments for You (Ridge & Aurora)

Book 7.5: A Wilder Wedding (Amos & Naomi)

Book 8: Forever For Us (Wyatt & Ava)

The Cage Family

Book 1: The Forever Rule (Aston & Emma)

The First Time Series:

Book 1: Good Time Boyfriend (Heath & Denver)

Book 2: Last Minute Fiancé (Luca & Addison)

Book 3: Second Chance Husband (August & Paisley)

The Montgomery Ink: Fort Collins Series:

Book 1: Inked Persuasion (Jacob & Annabelle)

Book 2: Inked Obsession (Beckett & Eliza)

Book 3: Inked Devotion (Benjamin & Brenna)

Book 3.5: Nothing But Ink (Clay & Riggs)

Book 4: Inked Craving (Lee & Paige)

Book 5: Inked Temptation (Archer & Killian)

The Montgomery Ink: Boulder Series:

Book 1: Wrapped in Ink (Liam & Arden)

Book 2: Sated in Ink (Ethan, Lincoln, and Holland)

Book 3: Embraced in Ink (Bristol & Marcus)

Book 3: Moments in Ink (Zia & Meredith)

Book 4: Seduced in Ink (Aaron & Madison)

Book 4.5: Captured in Ink (Julia, Ronin, & Kincaid)

Book 4.7: Inked Fantasy (Secret ??)

Book 4.8: A Very Montgomery Christmas (The Entire Boulder Family)

Montgomery Ink: Colorado Springs

Book 1: Fallen Ink (Adrienne & Mace)

Book 2: Restless Ink (Thea & Dimitri)

Book 2.5: Ashes to Ink (Abby & Ryan)

Book 3: Jagged Ink (Roxie & Carter)

Book 3.5: Ink by Numbers (Landon & Kaylee)

Montgomery Ink Denver:

Book 0.5: Ink Inspired (Shep & Shea)

Book 0.6: Ink Reunited (Sassy, Rare, and Ian)

Book 1: Delicate Ink (Austin & Sierra)

Book 1.5: Forever Ink (Callie & Morgan)

Book 2: Tempting Boundaries (Decker and Miranda)

Book 3: Harder than Words (Meghan & Luc)

Book 3.5: Finally Found You (Mason & Presley)

Book 4: Written in Ink (Griffin & Autumn)

Book 4.5: <u>Hidden Ink</u> (Hailey & Sloane)

Book 5: <u>Ink Enduring</u> (Maya, Jake, and Border)

Book 6: <u>Ink Exposed</u> (Alex & Tabby)

Book 6.5: <u>Adoring Ink</u> (Holly & Brody)

Book 6.6: <u>Love, Honor, & Ink</u> (Arianna & Harper)

Book 7: <u>Inked Expressions</u> (Storm & Everly)

Book 7.3: <u>Dropout</u> (Grayson & Kate)

Book 7.5: <u>Executive Ink</u> (Jax & Ashlynn)

Book 8: <u>Inked Memories</u> (Wes & Jillian)

Book 8.5: <u>Inked Nights</u> (Derek & Olivia)

Book 8.7: <u>Second Chance Ink</u> (Brandon & Lauren)

Book 8.5: Montgomery Midnight Kisses (Alex & Tabby Bonus(

Bonus: Inked Kingdom (Stone & Sarina)

The On My Own Series:

Book 0.5: My First Glance

Book 1: My One Night (Dillon & Elise)

Book 2: My Rebound (Pacey & Mackenzie)

Book 3: My Next Play (Miles & Nessa)

Book 4: My Bad Decisions (Tanner & Natalie)

The Promise Me Series:

Book 1: Forever Only Once (Cross & Hazel)

Book 2: From That Moment (Prior & Paris)

Book 3: Far From Destined (Macon & Dakota)

Book 4: From Our First (Nate & Myra)

The Less Than Series:
Book 1: Breathless With Her (Devin & Erin)
Book 2: Reckless With You (Tucker & Amelia)
Book 3: Shameless With Him (Caleb & Zoey)

The Fractured Connections Series:
Book 1: Breaking Without You (Cameron & Violet)
Book 2: Shouldn't Have You (Brendon & Harmony)
Book 3: Falling With You (Aiden & Sienna)
Book 4: Taken With You (Beckham & Meadow)

The Whiskey and Lies Series:
Book 1: Whiskey Secrets (Dare & Kenzie)
Book 2: Whiskey Reveals (Fox & Melody)
Book 3: Whiskey Undone (Loch & Ainsley)

The Gallagher Brothers Series:
Book 1: Love Restored (Graham & Blake)
Book 2: Passion Restored (Owen & Liz)
Book 3: Hope Restored (Murphy & Tessa)

The Ravenwood Coven Series:
Book 1: Dawn Unearthed
Book 2: Dusk Unveiled

Book 3: Evernight Unleashed

The Aspen Pack Series:
Book 1: Etched in Honor
Book 2: Hunted in Darkness
Book 3: Mated in Chaos
Book 4: Harbored in Silence
Book 5: Marked in Flames

The Talon Pack:
Book 1: Tattered Loyalties
Book 2: An Alpha's Choice
Book 3: Mated in Mist
Book 4: Wolf Betrayed
Book 5: Fractured Silence
Book 6: Destiny Disgraced
Book 7: Eternal Mourning
Book 8: Strength Enduring
Book 9: Forever Broken
Book 10: Mated in Darkness
Book 11: Fated in Winter

Redwood Pack Series:
Book 1: An Alpha's Path
Book 2: A Taste for a Mate
Book 3: Trinity Bound

Book 3.5: <u>A Night Away</u>
Book 4: <u>Enforcer's Redemption</u>
Book 4.5: <u>Blurred Expectations</u>
Book 4.7: <u>Forgiveness</u>
Book 5: <u>Shattered Emotions</u>
Book 6: <u>Hidden Destiny</u>
Book 6.5: <u>A Beta's Haven</u>
Book 7: <u>Fighting Fate</u>
Book 7.5: <u>Loving the Omega</u>
Book 7.7: <u>The Hunted Heart</u>
Book 8: <u>Wicked Wolf</u>

The Elements of Five Series:
Book 1: From Breath and Ruin
Book 2: From Flame and Ash
Book 3: From Spirit and Binding
Book 4: From Shadow and Silence

Dante's Circle Series:
Book 1: <u>Dust of My Wings</u>
Book 2: <u>Her Warriors' Three Wishes</u>
Book 3: <u>An Unlucky Moon</u>
Book 3.5: <u>His Choice</u>
Book 4: <u>Tangled Innocence</u>
Book 5: <u>Fierce Enchantment</u>
Book 6: <u>An Immortal's Song</u>

Book 7: <u>Prowled Darkness</u>
Book 8: Dante's Circle Reborn

Holiday, Montana Series:

Book 1: <u>Charmed Spirits</u>
Book 2: <u>Santa's Executive</u>
Book 3: <u>Finding Abigail</u>
Book 4: <u>Her Lucky Love</u>
Book 5: Dreams of Ivory

The Branded Pack Series:
(Written with Alexandra Ivy)

Book 1: <u>Stolen and Forgiven</u>
Book 2: <u>Abandoned and Unseen</u>
Book 3: <u>Buried and Shadowed</u>

About the Author

Carrie Ann Ryan is the New York Times and USA Today bestselling author of contemporary, paranormal, and young adult romance. Her works include the Montgomery Ink, Redwood Pack, Fractured Connections, and Elements of Five series, which have sold over 3.0 million books worldwide. She started writing while in graduate school for her advanced degree in chemistry and hasn't stopped since. Carrie Ann has written over seventy-five novels and novellas with more in the works. When she's not losing herself in her emotional and action-packed worlds, she's reading as much as she can while wrangling her clowder of cats who have more followers than she does.

www.CarrieAnnRyan.com

Made in United States
North Haven, CT
14 August 2025

71659346R00183